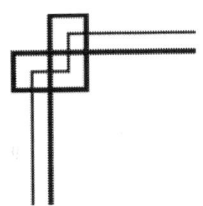

THE
ROZE ROYSS
FAMILY

J. L. Jones

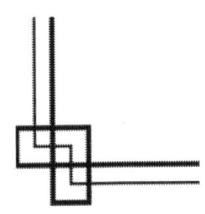
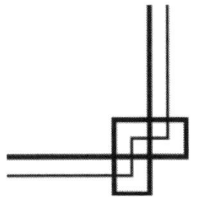

Copyright © 2022 by J. L Jones, The Roze Royss Family All rights reserved

First Edition

All rights reserved. This book or any portion thereof may not be reproduced or used in any manner whatsoever without the express written permission of the publisher except for the use of brief quotations in a book review.

The characters and events portrayed in this book are fictitious or are used fictitiously. Any similarity to real persons, living or dead, is purely coincidental and not intended by the author.

Book cover designed by Claire Julien, Claire.julien@ziggo.nl

Book formatted by Olivia Stone.

Printed in the United States of America.

Contents

Dedication 1
Acknowledgements 2
Prologue 4
Chapter 1 - Zaniyah Roze Royss 8
Chapter 2 - Ziola Roze Royss 14
Chapter 3 - Zander Roze Royss Jr 20
Chapter 4 - Zada Roze Royss 25
Chapter 5 - Zandell Roze Royss 34
Chapter 6 - Zandra Roze Royss 42
Chapter 7 - Zaniyah Roze Royss 48
Chapter 8 - Zander Roze Royss Sr 53
Chapter 9 - Ziola Roze Royss 60
Chapter 10 - Zada Roze Royss 64
Chapter 11 - Zander Roze Royss Jr 71
Chapter 12 - Zaniyah Roze Royss 77
Chapter 13 - Zandell Roze Royss 83
Chapter 14 - Zander Roze Royss Jr 91
Chapter 15 - Ziola Roze Royss 97
Chapter 16 - Zada Roze Royss 104
Chapter 17 - Zaniyah Roze Royss 114
Chapter 18 - Ziola Roze Royss 118
Chapter 19 - Zandra Roze Royss 125
Chapter 20 - Zander Roze Royss Jr 132

Chapter 21 - Zada Roze Royss 137

Chapter 22 - Zandra Roze Royss 148

Chapter 23 - Zandell Roze Royss 153

Chapter 24 - Zander Roze Royss Sr 156

Chapter 25 - Zandell Roze Royss 163

Chapter 26 - Zandra Roze Royss 172

Chapter 27 - Zandell Roze Royss 178

Chapter 28 - Zaniyah Roze Royss 184

Chapter 29 - Zandell Roze Royss 193

Chapter 30 - Zander Roze Royss Sr 205

Chapter 31 - Zada Roze Royss 211

Chapter 32 - Ziola Roze Royss 225

Chapter 33 - Zada Roze Royss 229

Chapter 34 - Zandell Roze Royss 236

Chapter 35 - Zada Roze Royss 247

Chapter 36 - Zandra Roze Royss 251

Chapter 37 - Zander Roze Royss Jr 257

Chapter 38 - Zandell Roze Royss 262

Chapter 39 - Zander Roze Royss Jr's Wedding 274

Chapter 40 - Zandra Roze Royss 282

Chapter 41 - The Letter 289

Chapter 42 - Zander Roze Ross Jr 296

DEDICATION

I dedicate this book, first and foremost, to myself. I've worked so hard, and I've finally made it. Secondly, I want to dedicate my book to my three children, Durnecia Bell, Zarious Bell, and Duran Bell Jr. My kids always motivated me on writing and cheered me on all the way to publishing. They always asked about my progress, and I love them to the moon and back! Mommy did it again!

ACKNOWLEDGEMENTS

I made it again! I want to acknowledge myself first for not giving up on my dreams and pushing through. I've made it to authorship! I am so proud and honored to let the world enjoy my writing, which is one of my true passions.

I want to acknowledge my true and dearest friend who's one of my number one fans and supporter, Christopher Mays. He made me write when I was too tired, he inspired me when I didn't know what to write due to writer's block or just simply, me wanting to give up. His advice was to simply write anything to get my writer's blood flowing and I did. I will always love him for consistently giving me the exact push that I need.

I want to acknowledge some people that continuously asked about my writing. They always showed excitement about my accomplishments. My cousins Nijeria Johnson, Tierra St. Felix and Shonda Watkins. I am giving a shout out to these beautiful and immaculate ladies because regardless of what they were going through or what was happening in their lives, they always took time out to talk to me about my endeavors. I appreciate them for always pushing me forward in this great writing journey. They are more excited than me. lol

One last person I want to give thanks to, my nephew Mark Mosley. You've always had my back with whatever goals I set forth. You loved how I would always fight against the grain and be different from the rest. I hate that you are not here to see what I am accomplishing today. I love you dearly. Rest in peace.

Lastly, I want to thank you all. All my current and future fans. Without you this would not work so you are my everything. I thank you for being here for me in supporting my dream. You're the best! Let's Read!

Prologue

Ziola

I stood before the minister in my stunning white wedding dress, with my hands clasped in my husband's. With adorning eyes lingering over his handsome and sweet brown face, my heart swelled with joy.

"You may now kiss your bride." The minister proudly announced.

With the tenderness of my now newfound husband, his lips pressing softly against mine, my skin began to crawl, my blood vibrated underneath by light velvety skin, and my heart fluttered; at that very moment, I knew I had found the love of my life. The kiss deepened, and the tightening feeling between my virgin legs created my juices to flow. I wanted to take my new husband right there and in front of everyone. However, I gently pulled away, and his scent was left on me and lingered in the air. Oh how I love this man.....

Wow-what a great memory. Ziola Roze Royss smiled to herself as she slowly awakened from her hypnotic, love-felt dream. Ziola looked to her right at her peaceful sleeping husband, Zander Roze Royss. He looked so angelic and powerful all the same time. Her smile started to fade away and was replaced with a look of pain and sorrow. Her mind went into fear mode just thinking about how this day would go.

Will he show me love and buy me gifts, will he ignore me, will I get cursed out, will I have to endure mental abuse, or will I be alone because he doesn't want to be around me, or………Ziola stopped thinking about the numerous ways her day could go. Honestly, she did not know. She turned her head to stare up at the fancy ceiling fan to watch it spin and spin…

"What are you doing?" Ziola yelled. Just that quick, he jumped up and startled her by wrapping his hands around her neck, choking her. Ziola grabbed his hands and clawed at them. She started to feel his knees force open her legs as he continued to tighten his hands around her neck. As she started to feel outpowered, she thought about the stars and how she will welcome heaven. She could imagine the heavenly gates with angels standing at the entrance as she walks through. Ziola came back to reality when she felt her husband's thick pulsating member, which felt good a lifetime ago, rip its way past her dry pink walls.

"I am here, heavenly father, take me," Ziola whispered out loud, her body limp.

Zander grunted and pumped with sweat dripping from his face. White thick foam formed in the corners of his mouth as he fucked Ziola in rage. She saw his white pearly teeth through his thick lips with bubbled spit oozing in and out. His foamed white bubbles started to splatter onto her perfectly made face and soft breasts. Ziola shut her eyes tight to pretend that she was in another place. She was in so much pain and wanted to die. As her eyes remained shut and the grunting got louder, her sweet soft spot became filled with her husband's horrible seed. She heard his last grunt. "Aghhhhhhhhhhhhhh! Bitch! You are a fucking whore!" She started to see a white flashing light, and then came darkness.

"How did I get here?" were Ziola's last thoughts.

"Zaniyah Roze Royss"

Chapter 1

ZANIYAH ROZE ROYSS

The Roze Royss family get together for dinner every Sunday. Its fuckin annoying.

I will give you the break down on our rich, cool, drama-filled and fucked up family. I have 4 other siblings other than myself. I am the middle baby and I see everything. I am twenty, in college studying dance. I am going to open my own dance studio for little girls one day. Also, I am simply the shit! Not one bitch got shit on me. I have my issues, but I have every reason to have them. You will find out soon enough. Enough about my lovely Goddess self, let's talk about my oldest brother. I have an older brother and his name is Zander Roze Royss Jr and he is a criminal attorney, he's an ole soft ass punk. He is the biggest goddamn momma's boy on earth. You wouldn't be able to tell if you didn't know him. He's one of the top attorneys in the South. Nobody fucks with my brother. He is the man. However, he loves his mommy. Booo Hooo…. He gives her whatever she wants. Yeah, yeah, yeah, I know what you're thinking. Well, that is his mother. Bitch, please. My mother? I can't stand that raggedy ass bitch! Yup I said it and what are you going to do about it! I'll wait……. Yup just as I thought, not a got damn thing!

Anyhoo, back to my whack ass brother. He loves his mommy to death, and I know he is her favorite as well, but she so-call don't show it. You know how mothers are. They always say how they don't have any favorites, but we all know that's a lie. Her favorite saying is that she gives her love to the child who needs it the most at that time. OK!! Yeah, right Bih! Moving on to my oldest sister with her dry as fuck ass. Excuse my language but this is how I talk so bitches get use to it.

My older sister is dry dry dry. She is quiet and to herself. She does everything right. I can't even talk about her because she is so great. She gives me money whenever I need it, which is never because my family is loaded, she gives me advise, she hides my secrets, and she is always there when I need her. She is my best friend. Also, she is a realtor for our father's company, she is the best in the South as well, not just Florida, the South. Her name rings bells and she do not play about her realty. However, there is something that puzzles me, and I haven't put my finger on it yet. She has a husband named Alexander Pierson and he owns Pierson Real Estate Company and sells million-dollar homes also, but he is not like the Roze Royss family. I think he's a bit jealous of my sister, but he tries not to show it. She has one child name Alexis, and she is the perfect wife. Even though she works, dinner is always cooked, the house is always clean, her daughter is always put together, and my sister always, always, always looks perfect. She wakes up with make up on. I do not know how she holds it down like that, but she does. I love her to the ends of the earth and back. I will hurt somebody over her. She is still dry as hell, don't party or get her swerve on but I love her so much.

My baby brother Zandell Roze Royss is 15teen, in high school and is popular than ever. He's already 6ft and is ballin! His basketball game is out of this world. He will be going to the NBA. Especially with daddy's connections. He is so handsome; all the girls want him. I told him to always have a condom on him just in case he wants to get into some of these girls' pants. Lol lol He laughs at me, but he takes the condoms anyway. He is a straight A student; you can't get no better than that. The boy is stella. I will fuck a bitch up behind that lil boy. All the kids in his high school know me. I will turn that muthafucka out!

Now on to my fast ass thirteen-year-old sister Zandra Roze Royss. That lil heffa is off the chain. She is one of those young conniving, manipulating, corrupted ass kids that will talk proper in your face and you will think she is the sweetest jewel but when she walks off, she has your wallet, draws and dick in her hand. Nutty ass lil girl. I wonder where she gets it from. Hmm O well, anyhoo. She is very smart and has great potential to be and do whatever she wants but she chooses to be bad as hell. She is always fighting and getting into trouble. Right before things get out of control and my parents begin to start taking things away from her, that lil bitch gets straight A's and becomes the world's best student. Crazy ass lil girl. I see straight through that ole demented ass chick. If somebody or a group of people was whipping her ass, I would let them. I might even give her a swift kick in her ass my goddamn self. My mother is blinder than a bat when it comes to her, and my dad just don't care. He just gives her whatever she wants to shut her up. Raggedy ass parents. And you wonder why we are all fucked up. Oh well, moving on. I'll briefly speak on my parents; I almost forgot about those scrubs.

My mom Ziola Roze Royss is like my sister. Perfect in every way. It's very fuckin annoying as well. She walks perfect, talks perfect, does her hair perfect, dresses perfect, you know what? She is just simply muthafuckin perfect. Her make-up is to perfection, and her hair is never out of place. I've never even heard my mother burp or fart. What kind of shit is that? I do stuff to piss her off, like pass gas at the table or burp loudly. I say excuse me, though. Damn. Don't judge me. Anyhoo, I do not like how she caters to my dad. It drives me insane. I can't stand when a woman just bows without question and doesn't stand up for herself. That's what it looks like to me. She needs to woman up. So, we get into it all the time. Also, she loves the hell out of my brother and talks shit to the rest of us, well, just my baby sister and me but who's keeping track. Don't get it twisted. Just because she bows only to my father, and she is perfect doesn't mean she won't ride your ass. Mrs. Ziola will do that, in fact, she loves to roast mines and my lil sister's ass every time she gets a damn chance.

Now, let's get to my dad. My sweet, sweet, sweet dad. Oh, how sweet he is. He gives money to everyone, and he works hard. My dad protects me from that beast of a mother of mines. Between him and my oldest sister, I can get away with anything. However, my father and I get into it because I don't like how he talks to my mother. I know, I know; I don't like her ass, but that is still my damn momma at the end of the day. Also, he hates that my brother is an attorney instead of running the family business. My brother and father get into it every Sunday at the dinner table. It's ridiculous. He is also mad at my brother for not already having a wife and kids. Boo Hoo! Dad, get over it already. My dad is cool with everyone else, but he is always angry, and the only thing I can think of is that when a person is angry like how my dad is, which is all the time, that means they are doing wrong, and they have something to hide. Hmm, I wonder.

So, it's time to move on so you can get the first glimpse of our Sunday dinners. This family gets on my goddamn nerves, but I love them. I guess.

"Ziola Roze Royss"

Chapter 2

ZIOLA ROZE ROYSS

The table was set while ivory candles burned, the elegance brought a sense of love and grace to the room. The ambiance carried happy and sad vibes of love and hate intertwined with the aroma of a home-cooked meal good enough for royalty. The table was adorned with a thick white tablecloth and a meal of ham, baked macaroni and cheese, collard greens, baked beans, potato salad, cornbread muffins, and a vanilla and chocolate cake. My family was all present on this beautiful Sunday afternoon. The sun shined bright as the birds cascaded across the light blue sky to find their destination. The radiant beams shone through the large windows and kissed everyone's skin. They had their heads bowed, and grace began.

"Our Father Who Art in Heaven……"

As my husband said the prayer, I thought how wonderful our family look right now. It's sad that they don't have a clue what I am going through. Lord, please just stop my heart right now. I know my son Zander Jr will miss me, but he will be alright. I just want to leave this earth. O my God. No, I mean all my kids will miss me. O Lord, I am so confused. Just take me, take me, take……

"Amen."

I realized that I'm still alive, well, and breathing, so I whispered.

"Damn you, God.

Ziola

"So, Zaniyah, how is school going? Are you still enjoying dancing, or have you changed your mind about helping your sister with the family business?"

"Mom, I think you should worry about your son over there and don't concern yourself…"

My daughter Zada sharply cut her sister off.

"Mother, I have the greatest idea. Why don't we take a family portrait? Us women can go shopping for everyone."

I wanted to cut Zaniyah in two with this damn butcher knife, but I'll settle with staring her ass down. She is lucky her sister chimed in.

"That would be nice, Zada. Where is your husband today? Working?"

"Yes, Ma, as usual, he will make it next week, though. He promised. The realtor company is starting to pick up a little bit. So, he has been busy."

"That's lovely, Dear. I am happy to hear that. So, when am I going to hear about you having me some more grandbabies?"

BOOM!

Zander SR banged his fist on the table to shut everyone up.

"Can everybody just shut the fuck up so I can eat in peace, please? All this stupid talk, just shut up!"

I hate him! I wish he would just die, right here, right now, just die, Satan!!

"Zaniyah is right. Think about your own son working for the family business and see if HE can bring us any grandchildren. Talk about that, Ziola." He was starting on Zander Jr.

"Are you gay? Huh? Just say it! Zander Jr!!"

"No, Sir I am not, but what if I was? What are you going to do about it, huh?"

I am so stuck; I should be taking up for my babies. Zaniyah started all of this. Daddy's little whore. That's all she is.

"Ma!" Zada snapped me out of my trance. "Yes, Dear?" I smiled forcefully.

"Dad left the table; he is calling you."

"Ok, I'll be right back."

I put down her napkin delicately. Without anyone knowing, shakingly, I walked up the stairs to our room. Ok relax, Ziola, you can do this. As I walked in, I heard a sound to my left. SLAP!

"What was that for?" I cried.

"Don't you ever talk to my daughter like that. You can get on that funky ass son of yours, but don't you ever talk to my daughter like that again. Do you hear me?"

He was so close to my face. I smelled everything that he'd just eaten this morning. Muthafucka!

"Yes, Sr."

"Now get up and lay your ass on the bed and open them legs. I wanna fuck."

My heart started to beat so fast. No, not again. I'm still sore from this morning.

"Zander, I am sore; can we wait until later when my body has healed a little bit?"

He ignored me and grabbed me roughly by the arm, shoving me onto the bed on my stomach. "I don't want that pussy of yours. I want that ass."

Tears started streaming down my cheeks. There was a knock at the door. Saved by the knock.

"Ma, are you and dad coming back down? We are waiting on yawl. I meant; we are waiting on you two. We're hungry."

I could have cried with relief that my baby Zandra came to my rescue. The family never eats without Sr at the table.

"Yes, baby, here we come." I tried to sound as happy as I could.

"Get up and fix yourself," Zander whispered. "And you better not take long." He got up to fix his clothes and walked out of the room.

I climbed off the bed and went to the bathroom to cover the bruise already showing on my face. Little do the kids know, bruises are why I wear make-up in the first place. I hate the shit, really. But I must do what I have to do. I would never let my babies know their dad uses me as a punching bag and sex doll. I don't know how we got here. We were so in love at one point. What happened? The attack was interrupted, but I am in trouble tonight. I feel like I'm dying inside.

"Zander Roze Royss Jr"

Chapter 3

ZANDER ROZE ROYSS JR

I hate that muthafucka. I am glad that stupid ass dinner is over. I swear I'mma fuck him up one day. I can't put my finger on it, but I know he is doing something to my mother. I will find out, and when I do, I will fuck him up.

"Lavender, I'm home!"

"What took you so long, Big Daddy?" That moaning type of talk got Zander Jr's dick hard. "Are you ready to sex me? I missed you."

"O yes, I am. Let me get cleaned up."

I went into the bathroom, looked at myself in the mirror, and shook my head at my reflection. I can't commit to a woman to save my life. I love them all, and from the looks of it, they love me too. If my mother knew what I was doing, she would kill me.

I grabbed one condom and changed my mind immediately. Shit, I'll need all of these. So, I decided to take the whole box. I walked in the room with nothing on. My 6-foot height and rock hard abs always pulled the ladies. My chocolate skin made me even more edible.

"Bend over." I ordered.

"With pleasure." She complied.

Lavender got on the bed and turned over and positioned her butt in the air just how I liked it. She arched her back so I could have my sweet way with her. I slid my member in nice and slow. Her juices are perfectly wet, just like it should be.

"Touch your titties."

She started to rub on her brown areolas and licked her lips as I pumped into her body.

"Mmmmmm give it to me harder, Zan."

I hated when people called me my father's nickname.

I grabbed her hair and pulled her face towards me.

"What the fuck did I tell you to call me?"

"I'm sorry, give it to me harder, daddy."

"Hell yeah, that's more like it! Bend that ass over."

The harder she cried out, the harder I pumped.

"Shut the fuck up!"

I grabbed her hair again and slid out. I needed to hurt something, so I slid into her ass.

"Damn, that ass feels good."

Lavender tried to deal with the pain by staying still. She was too scared to say anything; She didn't want to make Daddy mad.

"Kiss me."

She started kissing me as I fucked her from behind. She moaned in silence to the pain she was feeling. I didn't give a damn, I kept pounding her insides.

She started speaking.

"Yes, Daddy, give me that big dick. Hmmm hmmm."

Just how I like it.

"O my ass is so wet."

That was it. I was about to climax. I pushed her head down to the bed so I could go deeper in her ass. I started going crazy.

"Take this dick. Do you like it?"

"Yes, big daddy, I like it. Cum in me!"

"Aghhhhhhhhhh Damn, throw that shit back Bitch!"

"Like that?"

"Yes, O shit, like that. Damn!"

"Is that it, Big Daddy?"

"Yes, O yes. Fuuuuuuuuuuck!"

She fell to the bed, and I collapsed on top of her. Holding onto the condom, I withdrew. I tried catching my breath.

"Baby, are you ok?"

"Yes, I'm good. Here." I got up and threw her clothes at her. "Time to bounce. By the time I get out of the bathroom, you shouldn't be here."

Time to call my next bitch.

"Zada Roze Royss"

Chapter 4

ZADA ROZE ROYSS

I hate driving up to this place. Only because he's here. Him meaning, my husband. My family owns 15 acres of land, and all of us have our own mansions built on it. The land is so big that no one knows what the other person is doing. I love having my family in acres reach, just in case I need them. Well, that's what I thought before I got married. As I walk in the house, this drunk, lazy sack of shit is just sitting on the living room couch watching football. No one knows this, but his business isn't doing so great. My company is taking all their business, and our marriage is falling apart because of it. I am glad that my daughter is over at her friend's house tonight.

"So how was the Royal full of shit Sunday dinner?" He asked, laughing his stupid head off.

I wanted to knock the shit out of him. "My mother asked about you. And I told her you were working. You should probably come to the next dinner, or they will want me to have dinner here. You know you don't like it when they come here." *Because they can see you're the one that's full of ass cheeks.*

"I knew your mother would ask about me. You know she wants me." He slurred.

He is soooooo ignorant. "You don't even want you." I walked away.

"Fuck you bitch!"

"I sure will."

I already know that he would be asleep in a minute, so I'd just wait to sneak out later. We sleep in separate rooms, so when I change clothes and leave out at night, he doesn't know shit. I went to my luxury room and slipped out of my pencil skirt set that I usually wear to my parents' dinner. I changed into my hot red body-fitting one-shoulder drawstring dress. It's hiked up on one leg all the way up to my upper thigh with a string. I wore diamond-studded open-toe shoes, diamonds around my neck and in my ears. I had on a thousand-dollar diamond mask with my SuperStay Maybelline Matte shiny sparkled red lipstick. My hair was up in a tight neat French roll with a curl hanging loosely down the sides of my face. I am going to a Masquerade party. See, if that dumb ass husband of mine got it together, I would be home with him. But nope, I don't have it like that in this so-called marriage. So, I'll have fun all by myself. Well, not exactly. Hahaha.

The party is lit! The mansion is packed with ballers with masks on, and you can't tell who is who. Everyone is dressed to the nines. Money is everywhere. I pulled up in my all-white with butterscotch seats 2021 BMW 7 Series 740i. When I stepped out, all eyes were on me. My family don't know, but they should know that yo girl is the shit! I am a Roze Royss Bitch as my little sister always say. As I walked through the tall giant doors, I started to look around the mansion. I already knew who I was looking for. My song by Ms. Jonez Jody Macc, "Loving You Boy" came on, and I started dancing by myself. I danced slow, winding my hips to the beat. My exposed leg was getting more exposed. A person whispered in my ear from behind me to see if I wanted to dance, and I let him. I didn't even turn around to see how he looked or who he was. I just put my ass on his crotch and started slow grinding on him. His dick was so hard; he could have made this mansion blow. Hahaha, he started to rub on my arms, and that's when the fun went away. I didn't feel anything anymore, so I turned around to see where my big dick dancer went, and I was eye to eye with that familiar face.

"Are you serious? Have you lost yo got damn mind?"

Raphael LoveChild, AKA Ca$h. He's the number one artist in the country, and this is his mansion. He is my man, and I am in love with this rough-neck ass 6-foot Hershey chocolate drop. When I say fiiiiiiine, I mean it with every letter of the word.

"What babe? I was just dancing with him."

"No! You were dance-fucking him." He grabbed my hand, "Stay yo ass close to me. I can't take you nowhere. Damn it, man."

He can. I just do shit to piss him off. If my family knew what I was doing, they would kill me. I know I am living two lives but guess what, I don't give a fuck.

We met through my realtor company. I sold him this mansion and that's how we got started. The rest is history.

We continued to walk to his secluded area so we can be alone. I know he wanted to chastise me.

"Hello, Ms. Roze Royss."

The security guards know me. Everyone does. Everyone knows that I am Raphael's girl. So, Ca$h poured me some Rose' in my personal wine glass; he knew I was coming. He does these parties for me because he knows that I like to have fun. He put his arm around me and pulled me in close.

"Why are you always playing with me like that? You know I don't like that shit, Red." He only calls me Zada when he is mad, but any other time, it's Red.

He started twirling the curl dangling from my face around his finger.

"I'm sorry, baby. I didn't see you and I wanted to dance. I promise to be good for the rest of the night."

"Why didn't you wear your afro? You know that shit turns me on."

"I know, but I wanted to do something a little different. It took me forever to Stretch my hair and get it up in this French roll."

"I like it, but I like your real hair better. You know I love me some Red but don't let me fuck you up behind these raggedy-ass niggas. I can only deal with one muthafucka, and that's that stupid ass nigga at yo crib." He stared into my eyes with so much love. "Stop playing around with my emotions. Aight?"

"Ok. I got you. I'll stop doing crazy stuff."

"You know I love you, right?"

"I do. And you know I love you too, right?'

"I do." He smiled.

"How about I make it up to you," I whispered.

"O word? How?"

"Let me show you."

I stood and grabbed Raphael's hand and made him follow me. He looked so sexy with his black jeans, red and black polo shirt, topping it off with his red and black air force ones. Damn, he is sexy as hell. I had him wrapped around my finger, and vice versa. We started to walk down a corridor, and I know this spot all too well. This is where we had our first encounter. Tonight, I wanted him in his studio. It was lit up with red and lavender lights. Amplifiers, speakers, mics and beat machines lined up along his desk. I placed him in front of his chair, where he made his music. I played my favorite song, "The Elevator" by Ms. Jonez Jody Macc. I love her because she puts me in the right mode. I started to kiss him slowly as I unzipped his pants and dropped them to his ankles along with his briefs.

"Sit." I demanded.

"Mmm, Yes Ma'am." We took off our masks.

"Lay your head back and close your eyes. Just relax." He did as I instructed. I crawled my fingers along his penis with my right hand. I put my tongue delicately on the head of his shaft.

"Shit, I love that damn tongue, Red."

"Shhh, relax." He laid his head back again. I placed my mouth over his head slowly and sucked softly. He grabbed the arms of the chair as I placed his whole penis in my mouth. I changed my tempo and sucked at medium speed.

"Suck yo dick Red. Damn."

He put his hand on my head and I sucked a bit harder and faster. I began to lick up and down his shaft and sucked along the sides.

"O fuck."

I slid my panties off, got up and steadied myself on the head of his penis and I tightened my pussy walls as I slid down his shaft until he filled my walls completely.

"Red, I want this pussy forever. Shit. I love this juicy ass."

I started to grind as I moved up and down on his hard wet member. I wrapped my arms around his neck and sucked on his lips.

"Ca$h, do you like it?" I squeezed my walls tighter.

"Hell yeah. I love this shit."

"Say my name."

"Red. Shit, Red."

"No, my real name." I tightened my pussy walls more.

"Fuck. Zada."

"Nigga say my whole name!"

"Zada Muthafuckin Roze Royss!!!!"

I started to move up and down faster.

"I love it when you squeeze my dick like that. Damn Red, ride that shit,"

I started circling my hips, and he grabbed my ass with his massive hands and pulled me into him.

"Red, you so wet. Fuck."

I started kissing his lips again.

"Fuck. Shit. It's…. cumming… Red!"

Right before he came. I jumped off him and wrapped my lips around his dick and sucked the cum right out.

"What the fuck!!! O shit, o shit."

He shot his seed down my throat. It was warm and tasty. He wasn't expecting that. Hell, I wasn't either.

He was catching his breath, and I wrapped him in my arms as I sat in his lap.

"Red, I fuckin love you, girl. You will be my wife one day. I am not playing. So, when are you leaving that busta ass nigga?"

"Soon, baby, soon. No worries."

"Aight, if you need me to be there when you do it, I will. You know me, I'll fuck a muthafucka up about mines."

"I know, babe. I got it. Promise."

"Ok."

He kissed me with every piece of love in his body.

I finally got home at around 5 am in the morning. I didn't have houses to show today so it was just gonna be a lazy one. I walked by my spare room to see if the fucker was still asleep. And yes, I said my room because this mansion is mine. It's in my name. My father owns this property. My shitty husband gets nothing. But I know he will not go down without a fight. Don't judge me. I was a wonderful wife, I loved that man, gave him a daughter, and he messed it all up. I'll tell you about that later. Now I am going to lay with my man's scent on me and sleep. These joints are tired.

"Zandell Roze Royss"

Chapter 5

Zandell Roze Royss

Man, I am feeling really good. This year is almost over, and I will be a junior next year. College here I come. I can't wait to get out of this house. Yesterday was a disaster at Sunday dinner. Why does mom have to talk noise all the time? And why does dad have to use an iron fist all the time! They pretend like they have it all together, but they don't. I know things, things that ain't so pretty. My sister and I must live in this place they call a home. Well, I would love to help them with their problems, but I have problems of my own that needs fixing. School is mad hard. Keeping up with these straight A's is killin a brotha. I know, I know, you all are laughing at my problems but just imagine Zandell Roze Royss walking through the halls with his basketball in his hand, and he is a star player. Not any player but the type of player that colleges want right now. I am not supposed to be getting offers, but the colleges are calling me as we speak.

I am the youngest athlete with stardom potential. I am on ESPN. Smh. And to top it off, every girl on earth wants to get in my draws. I am a virgin, don't tell anybody and I'm not playin. Maaaaaan the honeys are riding my coat tail, and I can't get them off me. My mom keeps telling me to stay the hell away from them, and Zaniyah keeps giving me condoms. This life is torture.

My moms have been getting degrees behind my dad's back and telling me not to say anything, but I think she is setting herself up good so that she can leave my dad once and for all. I sure hope so. She is a housewife and does so much for that man, and he doesn't appreciate her. She also helps with his real-estate company. She's the best. I know I am 6 feet and a hundred and 180 pounds, but my dad is tough, so I am not ready for that fight just yet, but I feel that it will come one day. So back to the honeys, tell me what I should do? I don't want to date anybody; these girls are not the girls that I would want. They have weaves all the way down their backs, they're only in high school and their makeup is like they are on a runway, lashes are as long as my arm, and I think a few girls got their butt done. I can't. I want a natural girl who is kind, nice and warm.

"Hey, Zandell. I'm ready to see you play Friday. Are you going to the pool party on Saturday?"

"Well, um I don't know yet, but I'll let you know."

"Cool. I hope you do so I can show you how my bikini." She laughed with her home girls, blew me a kiss and walked off.

Maaaaaaaaaaan, she is a senior. Now do you see what I am saying. What am I supposed to do with that? You know what, I am not ready for college after all.

7th period begins.

"Aye, Zan! You going to the pool party Saturday? Man, it is going to be lit. All the bitches are gonna be there! I can't wait!"

My best friend Alex is so disrespectful. We have the same last period together, and he be straight tripping all day every day.

"Dang man don't call the women that. What is wrong with you? You all loud."

"Damn that; these girls love the disrespect. Watch this." He turned to a girl in our class.

"Aye Shonna, you gon let me hit that on Saturday?" He whispered.

"Hmm, I'll think about it. Are you going to bring me my starburst to the party like I asked?"

He nodded and threw her a wink. "Yeah, girl, you know I got you."

"Ok, then we will see, with yo sexy self." She winked at him and turned back to her class assignment.

"See, I told you that they are bitches. Man, I am going to tear that up."

"Ha you ain't gon do nothing with yo virgin self."

"Damn, man don't say that too loud. You gon mess up my reputation."

Alex is funny, and he loves the women. I wish I could be more like him, not afraid of girls and don't fall over my words whenever I'm in their company. Something is wrong with me.

After class, it's basketball practice. If I am not good at anything else, basketball is my Sh… you know the rest. I don't have to say it. As soon as I walked on the court, one of my teammates threw me the ball. I dribbled the ball in place, and my teammate started to block me. I held the ball to my left side, siked him out, went out, and faked to move to my right but went back to my left and ran down the court, bypassing everybody with my moves. There were two guys in front of me, so I just leaped, bringing the ball near the basket and used my right hand to bounce the ball off the backboard. SCORE!!! Two points for the team. I do not play. Ya boy is the MAN!

"Great job Zandell. Great job blocking guys, but you must stay close and up on him, got it?"

"Yes, Coach."

I know the guys hated constructive criticism, but that's what makes a person stronger. Smh these knuckle heads.

Practice came to an end, and this is when the kids go home and play games, get on the phone, talk to their girlfriends, friends, or be on some kind of electronic device. This is when the life of being a kid and enjoying your childhood happens. Well, not for me.

"How was school, Dear?"

Look at my mom. Behind that smile is tears, frustration, heartache, and anger. I feel for her, but she never tells us what she is going through, so how are we supposed to help? Poor mom. I love her so much.

"It was great, Ma. I hit'em with my famous layup today."

"It is Mother or mom, and you did what again?"

"I did a great job today at practice, Mother." I wanted to strangle her. There goes the I love you so much, mom.

"That's more like it, and I am glad to hear that, son."

"What's for dinner, Mom?"

"I had a lot of running around to do today, so I didn't have time to fix anything, so the chef will cook whatever you want."

My mother likes to cook with the chef. She says just because she is rich, that doesn't mean she can't be helpful.

"Do we have leftovers?"

"What?"

"Do we have leftovers, Mom?"

"You know what, yes, we do, you can help yourself to that if you'd like or have someone in the kitchen fix you a plate. I am going to lie down. Your Mother is exhausted."

"Ok, Ma, I mean Mother."

Now I see why my siblings act a fool. I went to the kitchen to fix my own plate.

"What you are doing?"

Got Dang It!! My sister Zandra scared the crap out of me!

"Hahahahaha scaredy-cat."

"Shut up. I am fixing something to eat. What do you want?"

"Are you going to the pool party on Saturday?"

"How do you know about that?"

"I know everything in this neighborhood or rather on this side of the earth. So, are you going or not?"

"I don't know yet, and why do you want to know?"

"I want to go with you."

"Your thirteen and Mom would kill me. Absolutely not."

"Everybody gets to have fun around here but me. I am going whether you take me or not. My boyfriend is going to be there."

"What??? Boyfriend? Ha! Yeah right. If I wanted to take you, I am surely not taking you now. You talk too much, and you tell everything. I also know you are having sex."

"Shhhhhhhhhhhh!! Omg really? Be quiet stupid! I use protection, so I am good. What about you, Mr. I Am Scared of Girls!"

"Shut up. Ok, if you want to come with me, you can't have sex, and you must stay with me where I can see you. You are not making babies on my watch. The first time you disappear, I will embarrass you to a whole new level, and then we are leaving. You know how I get down."

"Ok, I promise."

"Also, stay the hell away from the basketball team. You already look older than your age with all that gook in your hair and those clothes you be wearing that mom doesn't know about. Don't play with me, Zandra, and I mean it. Stay away from the ballers, do you hear me?"

"Yes. I hear you."

I love my little sister, but she is hot in the pants. I know she will sneak off to the party on her own, so I'd rather be with her than have her there alone. No telling what she will get into. O well, I guess I am going to the party. Smh

"Zandra Roze Royss"

Chapter 6

ZANDRA ROZE ROYSS

Haahahah I got his ass. My brother doesn't know a fool from a frog. I am going to turn that party out. I cannot wait; I know exactly what I am going to wear.

RING

"Yo, what's up, Red."

"Hey, Devin. I was calling to see if you can get out tonight?"

"What time, Shawty?"

"I can be at the front gate at midnight. Cool?"

"Hellz yeah. I'll be there."

"See you soon. Bye." Click! He hates when I hang up in his face. Boy, please, I got his ass whipped. This little coochie of mines is bussin. He doesn't want to mess with me and lose this good stuff right here. I know yawl are thinking that I am too young, but like Keith Sweat said, you may be young, but you're readyyyyyyyy. Hahahahaha. Straight up. I got to get ready for my midnight snack. Let's see, I will wear my black mini halter dress for easy access. O yawl didn't know? You better ask somebody. I have been doing this since I've been 10. Chile boo. I am experienced. My boyfriend is eighteen, and he knows what he is doing too. So, I know what I am talking about. Anyway, my hair is long, and down to my back, he likes to pull it, so I'll wear a ponytail. I am 5ft and weigh 125 pounds so he can handle all this, don't judge me.

Knock Knock....

"Who is it?"

"Daddy."

"Hold on, dad."

Zandra threw her nightgown over her halter dress and climbed into bed.

"Come in!"

"Hey, how is daddy's baby girl doing?"

"Oh, I am doing fine, Dad."

"Why are you in bed so early?"

"I'm tired. Volleyball practice was heavy."

"How are you doing in practice?"

"It's great Dad, I know I am going to probably go pro. My Coach said that I have a gift."

"Of Course, you do. You are the daughter of a Roze Royss. Ha-ha"

I love my daddy; he does nothing wrong in my eyes. He is the best and gives me whatever I want.

"That's right, daddy." I smiled. He needs to get the hell out of my room. I need to shave my cha-cha.

"Well, have a great night and get some rest. I'm looking forward to your game on Thursday."

"Me too."

My dad always comes to my and Zandell's games. He never went to any of the other kids' games. Maybe he was just simply too busy with his business or just don't like them, but whatever the reason was, who cares. He loves me. Selfish right! Hahahaha

"Good night, Daddy."

"Good night, baby girl." He kissed me on the forehead.

Zandra set her alarm for 11:45 pm to drive her dad's car to the front gate. She shaved her cha-cha, freshened up, then laid down to catch a nap.

ALARM SOUNDS

Dang, 11:45 pm got here quick. She jumped up and brushed her teeth, walked slowly down the hall and of course, as usual, she heard her nasty parents getting it on. Her mother is always sounding like sex hurt. O stop it, it hurts. Why are you hurting me like that, slow down, and her grunts are just unattractive. My father sounds like he be tearing it up. You go Dad! I finally got to the back stairs, got outside, and jumped in the car. I immediately turned off the lights. I started to drive and right when I was almost at the front gate, I saw someone. I pulled the car out of sight. Good thing I always drive daddy's black corvette, it's small and can move out of sight quick. Wait! Is that my sister Zada? Her married ass should be in bed. She was getting out of a tented hummer, and she slobbed a dude down. Holy SHIT!!!! That's that artist called Ca$h!!!! My married quiet ass proper talking sister is smashing a celebrity!! I can't wait until she pisses me off so I can throw this up in her face. However, her husband is a crab, so right on sis! I watched her tip toe to her car and drive to the back toward her property. Damn! It says CA$H on the license plate. Wow. I'm speechless. I drove the rest of the way to the front of the property and my boo was in our hiding place. I pulled up beside his 2021 beamer and hop out, sliding in his passenger seat.

"Hey, baby."

He grabbed my face with his hand.

"Didn't I tell you about hanging up on me? You know I don't like nor play that shit. Don't do it again."

"Ok, baby I'm sorry. It won't happen again." He let me go, and we grinned at each other. I wrapped my arms around his neck and slobbed him down.

"Oh, I love it when you play gangsta."

"You like that, huh?" He started to lay my seat back and pull up my dress. I had on no panties. His fingers did their dance on my clean and shaved cha-cha.

"Talk strong to me again." We started kissing wild.

"Don't hang up on me like that again, or I'll come over here and put this pipe on you hard, Bee."

"Yes, o yes. Spank me, Master Devin. Spank me." He turned my body to the side and started slapping my ass. He loves my curves and my nice rump. He positioned himself in front of me. He bent his head down and opened my legs wide before diving right in. I grabbed his head as he moaned and went wild.

"O yes, baby, lick it."

"Mmmmm, I got to get in it. Open wide."

I spread my thick legs as far as they could go. Devin was ready to enter with his penis covered with our favorite strawberry-flavored condom. Oooooo I love this part. I laid the seat all the way back, and Devin got on top. He is so amazing.

"Yeah, baby, do you feel that?"

"Oh yes, I can."

I really couldn't. He is reeeeeeally small and can't screw a tub if he was sitting in it already. His little pumps he was giving me wasn't doing a damn thing; I laughed inside. Look, I am fine with that. I don't need anybody trying to bust it wide open. I love his fine ass and this beamer. That's all I'm thinking about. He got money.

"Yes, my Master, you are working it."

I have to keep him entertained. He will be done in 3,2,1......

"Aghhhhhhh yes, my sweet baby. You made me do it."

He rolled back over to the driver's side and was out of breath like he ran a whole goddamn marathon. Hahahahaha. Non-sex having ass, but cute.

"Ok Devin, I have to go. No more role-playing. I have school in the morning."

"Ok, peach drop. I'll see you later. Oh yeah, and I can't go to the party with you this Saturday. Something came up. But I want you to be good. Don't let me hear that you did some fucked up shit."

"Man, please, I am just going to chill with the girls and hang out with my brother. That's it."

"Well, have fun, and I'll try to catch the next one. Cool?"

"Cool." I kissed Devin goodbye and hopped out of the beamer and skipped to the corvette, turned it on, immediately turned off the lights and drove back to the Roze Royss mansion. I crept through the unlocked back door and tiptoed to my room. Sliding my tired ass out of that tight dress, I threw my nightgown on and laid under the covers. Wow, I really needed Devin to come to the party because I have the biggest crush on the basketball team's co-captain at my brother's school. He is always liking my post and sending me messages through my social media accounts. It's crazy because dude is sweatin me hard. I try to stay away from him, and by Devin being there, I would have. Yo girl is trying to be faithful.

Chapter 7

ZANIYAH ROZE ROYSS

Looking up at the ceiling and thinking about my life. I am rich, and I have a big family. My plan is to own my own dance studio for young girls. I plan on making sure that I am that sound heart that pushes them to be the best they can be by not letting no one stand in the way of their dreams. I wish I had someone to do that for me. I never had support from the one person I truly need support from. My mom. Come on, she is no support of mines, my father is, and he gets on my nerves as well, but I want my mother to be there for me like I see other mothers be there for their daughters. I wonder why she hates me so much; I never did anything to her but be her daughter. I never asked to be here; it was her and my father's idea to put me here. I am so glad I do not stay in that house anymore. I feel sorry for my younger two siblings. Smh. I must be my own support system and take it one day at a time.

I looked over at Keisha to my right. She is the prettiest brown skin chick I have ever seen. She reminds me of the chick off that movie with DMX called "Belly." I reached over and rubbed her soft brown face, and she slowly moved to my touch. I smiled just slightly, but I could tell she was still sleep. She looks like an angel. I moved close to smell her hair. She wears the biggest afros, and her hair smells like almonds and coconut. I played in her hair for a little bit, and I had to kiss her soft lips. Damn, she looks tasty. I started to move close to her to take in her juicy bottom lip until he pulled up behind me and started rubbing on my titties. I like me some women, but I love me some men, damn that.

"You awake."

"Yes, Babe." I whispered to him.

I closed my eyes for a second to feel the excitement forming between my legs. I turned to my left, looked him in his eyes and forgot all about Keisha. He understands my fetish with men and women, and he don't mind. He said he will be here with me until I only want him. Hey, I get the best of both worlds, and honestly, he does too. I let him fuck the shit out of Keisha and me. Only us two. If he touches someone else, I will erase him. Seriously.

I started to kiss him slowly at first, then I moved to sit on top of him. He was ready as usual. He put his hand on my ass and guided me to his massive penis. Keisha started to move a little but stayed asleep. His name is Money, and his father is a celebrity. My parents hate when we find ourselves messing with artists, but I see nothing wrong with it. They make money, and we make money, period.

"Ride me, good Ma."

"Anything for you, Money."

I sat up on his body and positioned myself over his penis and slid down so effortlessly.

"Damn, I love this morning pussy. You are so wet."

"Mmmm Hmmm."

Keisha woke up and gave me a look. I knew what it meant.

"No, not this morning. He is all mines. Lay there and shut the fuck up or get the fuck out."

She stayed still and shut the fuck up. I know that I am being rude to her, but I don't like that look she gives when she doesn't want to see Money and I do what we do. Bitch, please.

I went back to performing my magic on Money's ass. I laid my hands flat on his tatted chest and looked him dead in the eyes. I twirled my hips and squeezed on his manhood so good he was crying out.

"Damn baby, I like it when you do that shit."

I started to move in an upward motion. Up and down and up and down. Our juices sounded off in the room. Keisha started paying with herself as she watched. I looked over at her with her pretty ass.

"Keisha, kiss me."

Just as the doctor ordered. She started kissing me, and I rode Money even harder.

"Fuck me, Zan. Damn girl. Yawl looking sexy as shit."

Keisha started sucking on my D cups while Money grabbed my hips and slammed his penis inside me.

"O my goodness. What the fuck."

Money and Keisha worked on me so well. I came 3 times.

"Keisha, that's enough. I have to finish this."

I pushed her ass back down on the bed and focused on Money. His tattoos and 8-pack always drive me crazy. I bent to kiss his lips, and I continued to work my hips. I started to bounce up and down; he loves this.

"Zan, I'm about to cum."

"Cum in me, Money! Cum baby."

"O shit!!! That's it!"

He filled me up with warm milky cream.

"Come here, Zan." He pulled me into his chest, and we all fell back to sleep just like that.

"Zander Roze Royss Sr"

Chapter 8

ZANDER ROZE ROYSS SR

Pulling up in my Bentley to a beautiful home in Carrollwood, Fl, I smiled brightly and thought nothing could stop me. I parked in the circular driveway and got out. I unlocked my house door and I smiled even brighter when Beverly greeted me.

"Hello, my King."

"Hello, my Queen."

We shared a loving and soft kiss that would make anyone want to cry. The love we have for each other is magical. Oh, how I love this woman.

"Hey, Dad!"

My 16-year-old triplets yelled out to me as they came out of the kitchen on their way to the door to leave for school.

"What's up, Roze Royss Crew." I hugged every one of them.

"Are you all ready for school?"

"Yes, Sir." They said in unison.

"Ok, cool. Get in the car. I'm coming. Start the car, Zachary and do not let your sister do it. You know she will try to drive."

"I'm on it, dad. I got you."

They shared a chuckle, and the triplets ran out to the car to get it started.

"Baby, you look stressed. What's wrong, my love?"

"It's nothing. I have a lot to do today but just seeing your face always makes me happy." I smiled down lovingly at this beautiful woman of mine.

"Ok, well, in that case….."

She kissed me again but with more passion this time. Her hand reached between my legs and massaged my penis.

BEEP BEEP!!

We bumped heads and started laughing.

"I have to go, but I will see you later, ok?"

"Ok, Love. What do you want for dinner?"

"Ummm, surprise me. Love you." I kissed her on her forehead, then kneeled to kiss her small round baby bump.

"Awwww, how sweet, and I love you too." She patted his butt, watch him get in the Bentley and waived as they drove off. Such a picture-perfect of a family.

"So, kids, how's school going?"

"Dad let's cut to the chase. Why don't you stay home with Mom and us?"

This is my mouth ole mighty daughter Zahara talking mess just like her sister Zaniyah. You know the one. Ms. College-wants-be-a-dance-teacher.

"Well, sweetheart, you see……."

"Dad don't lie. We know that you have another family."

I slam on the brakes, almost running the car off the road.

"What?" I gasp.

"Dad! Are you trying to kill us?" Zachary yelled. He is right in the front seat. He would have been the first to go to heaven with how I almost ejected him from the car.

"Yup, just so he doesn't have to worry about giving us no life insurance money when he dies. Be careful Zachary. He's trying to take us out!"

"Now stop that kind of talk Zahara. That is enough." I pulled the car over on the side of the road to focus and find out what in the hell does she know.

"Zahara, who told you that I have another family?"

"You did."

"Huh? I never told you that." My sons were looking back and forth like they were at a tennis match. I guess they had no idea what Zahara was talking about. Hell, I didn't either.

"Dad, you told me when you were here yesterday. I came outside to get something out of your car and there was a pink notebook that was on the floor back here with a "Daddy's Little Girl" keyring on it with a picture of you and a little girl. She looks just like me." Zahara folded her arms like she dared me to lie.

"Zahara…"

"Does she even know about us? Wait, does mom know?"

My head instantly pounded with all the difficult questions being thrown at me. What in the hell? This is why he locks his car doors because of shit like this.

"Zahara, baby girl…"

"O no you don't. You already have one of those.' She folded her arms even tighter. It looked like tears were forming. I am a sucker for my daughters.

"Ok, I promise to talk to all three of you after school, ok? Daddy promise. So, let me explain then we can go from there? Please say this is cool. Do not tell your mother. Let us talk first." I saw hesitation. "Please?"

"I know what school she goes to, and I am going up there to see her. How about that?"

"O no you are not! And that is final. I will talk to you three after school." I raised my voice this time. This is getting out of hand. My son Zanar was quiet the whole time until now.

"How old is she?" Zanar quietly asked.

"She is thirteen."

That's when Zanar broke his silence and said what was on his mind.

"So, let me get this right? You had a child with another woman thirteen years ago, and you have been raising her just like you have been raising us and you kept her a secret? You've been around my mother like we are a happy-go-lucky family, and you have been frontin this whole time? You cheated on my-now-pregnant- mother, and you are asking us to stay quiet, not to say a word to our innocent mother until you basically, dig your persuasive words into us first and talk us into not telling her? Are you serious? You got the hardest girl I know in this back seat about to cry; you got my talkative brother quiet, and you expect me to not say nothing to my mother? I'm sorry partna, but that ain't happening. Nobody disrespects my family."

My son stared me down.

It felt like steam was pushing out of my ears with how pissed I was. If these weren't my kids, I would have went off. However, Beverly is hood, but with class and she raised our kids that way. So, I can't use the iron fist with them like I can with my other kids unless I have to. And I guess I have to.

"Is this why you haven't put a ring on my mother's finger? Maaaan take me to school. I'm ready for school to be over with! So, I can get home and tell my momma what kind of a fucking loser of a dad you are!"

I reached in the backseat and grabbed Zanar's collared shirt, which made him start choking. Zahara and Zachary grabbed my arms to try and remove my hands.

Zanar punched me square in the face, so I let go of Zanar's shirt with a look of amusement. I couldn't believe my son squared on me like that. I was pissed but, damn, I was proud too.

Zanar jumped out of the car and put up his set.

"Come on! What's up?" Zanar threatened.

The boys are big like me, so I have to get my mind right. My boys are 6'1 and I'm 6 feet, my genes are strong as hell. My daughter is 5'7 and if I don't play my cards right, they will kick my ass.

Zahara grabbed the bookbags and hopped out after her dad while Zachary fell suit and ran up to Zanar to hold him back.

"You wanna try me Lil boy! Come On!"

"Daddy, are you crazy? You're going to fight your own son?" Zahara yelled, trying to hold me back.

"Hell yeah!"

"Look, we will walk to school! Yawl doing too much! Calm down, Zanar!" Zahara yelled.

"Man, fuck this! I'm out! You can have yo other family!" Zanar stormed off, and Zachary was right behind him.

"Come on, Zahara! Let's go!" Zachary shouted.

"I'm sorry, Dad, I gotta go. You really messed up this time." Tears fell from her eyes, and she turned and ran to catch up with her brothers.

Chapter 9

ZIOLA ROZE ROYSS

"Hello, delivery for Ziola Roze Royss. Please sign." I smiled and signed my name on the dotted line to receive my dozens of white tulips. Awwwwww, somebody thought of me today. I felt good about that. I limped back to the living room chair due to my sprained ankle. Zander was rough with me last week, but for some reason, he has been so kind and quiet lately. He didn't even come home a couple of nights this week. Thank goodness, I don't care where he is and what he is doing or who he is doing, for that matter. My sprained ankle is healing. My vagina and ass haven't been tampered with all week. I looked at my card attached to my flowers, and it was from Zander Sr. Huh? Wait, not Jr? No, it says Sr.

I had to brace herself when sitting. I read the card.

I know that I haven't been the nicest husband to live with, but I am going to do my best to make it up to you. Your loving Husband Zander Sr. What? Oh no. I hate you, you son-of-a-bitch. I am going to be out of here and your life as soon as possible. I love you Zander Sr, but you are a piece of shit!

Ding Dong

Really. Omg! The staff was off today. I sent everybody home until Zander comes back. I think he has them spying on me. I slowly got up and walked to the door. I saw right through the glass and shook my head. Then I opened the door to my daughter Zandra.

"Where is your key?"

"I forgot it, Ma. Are you ok? You have been getting hurt a lot lately."

I waved at the car pulling out of the driveway.

"I am fine, and why did Tiffany's mom drop you off so early from school?"

"Well, someone in class supposedly was tested positive for covid, so I must quarantine for 2 weeks. You will get a call in a few from the assistant principal."

". Let me call the school. Go upstairs and get settled."

"Ma, I want to ask you about this Saturday. Be right back." Zandra ran up the stairs.

I called the school and the covid story was true. I have to watch Zandra because that conniving little girl is sneeeeaky.

"Ok Ma...."

"Ummmm, excuse me?'

"O yeah, I meant, Mother, there is a party this Saturday, and I know you may want the house to yourself since daddy is gone.

So, can I go to the party with Zandell? Please? He is going and said he would keep an eye on me while I am there."

"Zandra, you are thirteen, and your brother is fifteen. This party doesn't sound suitable for you, my Dear."

"Mother, this is the party of the year. I have to be there."

"Who do you know is going to this party, and how do you even know about this party, Zandra?"

"Tiffany will be there with her big brother, and he's bringing his little sister as well. Oh please, mom. I won't ask you for anything else."

"Again, excuse me?"

"Ok, Mother, please let me go. I will be in good hands."

"I don't know. Give me a day to think about it, and I will also talk to your brother."

"Ok. Cool. I mean, thanks, mother." Zandra got up and went upstairs. "I'll be up here doing my work. You can go back to your housewives of Atlanta show. Hahaha."

How did she know that? I had the TV turned off when I went to answer the door. See, that's why I want to just be by myself, so nobody will know what I am doing in my spare time.

Ziola turned back on her show, and the phone rang.

"Hello, who's speaking?"

"Hello, Ziola?"

"I'm sorry, who's speaking?"

"Hello Ziola, you don't know me, but my name is Beverly, the mother of Zander Roze Royss's children?"

I sat for a moment, frozen like the Gods has just given me a wonderous gift. I chuckled and said,

"I'm sorry what's your name and who are you again?"

Chapter 10

ZADA ROZE ROYSS

I awakened to the pleasant sound of birds and the sun brightly glowing through the large window of my bedroom. I looked to my left and saw the specimen of a beautiful man lying beside me. Wrapped in his arms, I felt love like no other, which brought me to think about all of what I have sacrificed to be here right now. This is love that I never knew existed, or rather, love I thought I had. I smiled gently and started to softly kiss the side of his neck. He moaned that deep baritone sound. I moved my hands under the cover to caress his manhood, and his moan got louder, my pace quickened, I felt the precum squeeze into my soft hands. Mmmmmm, I'm so thirsty.

"Damn, baby." *His voice turned me on.*

I bent down under the covers and engulfed him into my wet mouth. I licked and sucked him until his eyes rolled to the back of his head. His penis tasted like a strawberry jolly rancher. He grabbed the sheets, and I knew he was about to release down my throat, so I changed my flow and started sucking on his delicate balls. He couldn't take it anymore, so he grabbed me and flipped me on my back. He kissed me wild and rubbed on my sweet spot so lovingly.

"Mmmmm, don't stop."

He positioned himself over me, covered my whole body with his strong chocolate one, and entered my sweet wet center with one quick motion. My breath caught in my throat. I closed my eyes as he worked his magic in me.

"Zada, say my name."

"Raphael." *I whispered.*

This excited him, and he began to pump harder into my sweet hole of lust.

"Say it again."

"Raphael," *I said a bit louder.*

And his rhythm quickened to where I couldn't contain myself any longer.

"Keep it right there. I feel it coming, yes, yes…" *I was almost there, and then just out of the blue, his face changed.*

"Bitch, get yo ass up."

"What the hell." *I looked at him like he was crazy.*

"I said get yo ass up Bitch!"

I jumped out of my sleep with sweat dripping down my face. And a puddle between my legs. That muthafucka woke me up by calling me a Bitch. Really? I hate his stinking ass.

"Are you taking our daughter to daycare or what, or did you forget that you had a child? She's downstairs waiting on you. I told you I am showing a house this morning, and I can't do it."

"Here I come. My bad."

"Your bad, all right. You were moaning, huh? Were you giving up the cat because you are damn sure not giving it up to me? Was that a man whore you were dreaming about?"

"Fuck you, Alex. And I heard you call me a bitch. Yo, momma is a bitch." I spat at him.

"Hahaha, she sure is. Now get up." He snapped.

"I said here the hell I come. Get out of my room!"

His dumb ass smirked and walked away.

That mutha….. oooooo he makes me sick. That's why I am giving up the cat. Hahaha asshole.

"Mommy's coming!"

I dropped her off and headed back home to put some clothes on and enjoy the day. I had no houses to show, and I was damn well happy about that. It is Friday, and I have a free night to just relax. Netflix and wine.

RING

"What's up, Red. What's happening?"

"Hey, sexy. Nothing, I just dropped my daughter off, and I am headed home to relax and chill."

"That's cool. Can I see you for a minute? I want to give you something."

"Ok, I have to put some clothes on, and I'll stop by."

"No need, I'm at your crib already."

"What?"

"Yup, I am parked outside the estate."

"Raphael, really! What the hell!"

"Oh, there you go right there. I see you."

CLICK

This crazy ass man got out of his white Benz and leaned against it like it was nothing. I was goddamn furious.

"Red hop in so I can get me a piece right quick."

What the fuc…

"Are you crazy? You can't come to my house like this, Raphael. My whole family lives here; including my damn parents. You need to leave now!"

"Not until you give me my ass. And damn, you look so sexy in that robe. What are you wearing?"

I was looking like a hot goddamn mess, and he was trying to be funny. But I laughed inside because he is hilarious.

"Come on, and let's make this quick. I am so mad with you right now that I can't even see straight."

"Come on, Red. Hurry yo ass up."

I rushed to the back seat of the car, and he followed. His pants were down with the quickness.

"Damn you look sexy with that robe on. I want you to sit on it. I miss you, Red."

"Listen, first off, be quick and secondly, promise me you will never come here unless I ask you to. Please."

He nodded. "Yeah, I got you. Now sit on it."

I took off my lace panties from under my silk nightgown and did exactly what the doctor ordered. He was ready too. I slid down his thick rod, and of course, my body was wet from the time he said he was at my house. Surprisingly, that shit turned me on.

"Damn, I'm loving this morning gush."

My juices sounded off in the car as I sucked in his member with my wet suction cup. He grabbed my ass with his hands and guided me up and down shaft. I squeezed on his dick good because I had to make this quick.

"Raphael, you feel so good."

"You do too baby."

I moved my hips in a circular motion as I squeezed on his penis. I grabbed his face and kissed the hell out of him like it was the last kiss we would ever have. I sucked on his tongue as I rode him. He loves my soft lips.

"Damn Red, I love it when you kiss me like that." He said in between kisses.

"Mmmmm hmmmm."

I began to pick up the pace and started bouncing up and down.

"Keep doing that shit, Red."

"You like it?"

"Hell yeah."

"Say it."

"I love it. Oh, I love it."

"You love it, huh?"

"Damn, I'm about to cum."

"Cum for me, baby."

"Oooooooo damn, Red!"

My baby busted his nut all inside of me. His semen felt so good and warm. Thank goodness for birth control.

"Ok, love you and I have to go. I must clean up for real now."

"Ok."

As we got dressed, I had to remind him again.

"Love, please don't come back here unless I ask you, ok?"

"I got you, Red. My bad, I just had to have you. I need you by my side every night, Zada."

I looooooooove when he says my name. That is when he is serious and speaking from the heart.

"Baby, it will happen. I just need time. I will talk to my brother soon about helping me with the separation, ok? Promise."

"Ok, you know I got lawyers too. And I pay them muthafuckas well."

"I love you."

"You know I love you too, Ma." He popped kiss me and patted me on my ass. I hurried up, hopped my behind out of the car to tighten my robe. I was so caught up in my scandalous ways that I did not see the eyes on me the whole time.

Chapter 11

ZANDER ROZE ROYSS JR

Today is Friday, and I am so happy. I am ready for the weekend to get started. I need this meeting to be over with asap. I have a few women coming over to wine and dine me. Yes, I love me some women. However, there is one woman that I am in love with for real. I would marry her today, and I can honestly say I would be faithful. She is a divorce attorney, one of the best in the South. She is smart, courageous, funny, has a sense of humor, and sexy as hell. She is a dime piece for sure. We dated for six months, and my dumb ass cheated on her. Hey, she wasn't giving up the goods. She is still a virgin to this day. Really! At the age of 25. How long can a brother wait? And yawl knows that I love the ladies. Well, she fell hard for me, but when I fucked up, I crushed her heart. As far as I can tell, she still loves me, but she is afraid, and I understand. I heard she is dating, and it's serious. That's what I heard.

"Good morning, Noel, how are you this lovely afternoon?"

"Hi, and I am great."

I can tell it took everything in her to smile and not cuss me out. Every Friday I see her. We always have a meeting at the courthouse to go over rules, regulations, and stipulations, you know, all the boring stuff. I just sit and stare at her. She is about 5 feet 4 inches, 145 lbs. with the prettiest gray eyes. She's light skin with light brown hair; curly like that wet and wavy hair the women buy in the hair stores. She's black, but her grandmother was Indian, and I mean a Cherokee Indian, and she loved her a black man. Her hair is down to the middle of her back. She is thick in all the right places. You can tell what she is working with when she wears those pencil skirts like the one, she has on today with her fluffy shirt and blazer. You can see her physique, but I know it all too well. I did strip her down to her panties and bra once

After the meeting was over, the lawyers proceeded toward the doors to leave, and I had to say something to her about how I feel.

"Noel, wait up." I jogged up to her. Surprisingly, she stopped for me.

"Yes? What's up, Zander?"

Ok, straight to the point. I get it.

"I was wondering if you would like to go to lunch with me. I need to talk to you. It's important."

"Ok."

Woooooow I can't believe it. I touched her elbow and directed her to my car.

We quietly drove down to Ybor in Tampa. We went to a restaurant called Columbia, got a table for two and sat by the window. The view was beautiful, watching folks enjoy their lives in this lovely weather. People sitting on benches, laughing, holding hands, even kissing.

"So, Noel, how is life treating you?" I asked, leaning forward.

"Let's cut to the chase, Zanny. What do you want?"

The waiter walks up right at that moment while my penis got hard by the way she called me Zanny. I love it when she calls me that.

"What can I do for you today?" The pretty young woman said. We both said," Water with no lemon."

The waitress looked at both of us a bit crazy.

"Ok, I'll be right back with your order."

She walked away, and I guess Noel thought that I had my eyes on her, so she got upset immediately.

"Why did you bring me here? Obviously, you haven't changed, and you want whatever I am not giving, so what do you want with me already?"

"I was not looking at that girl like that. I was just laughing inside at how she looked when we ordered our water. That is all, I swear."

"Ok fine. Now tell me why I am here."

"Ok, first I want to start out by saying that I miss you and I am so sorry. Wait before you say anything; let me finish, please." She sighed heavily and nodded for me to continue. "Ok, so I want you to know that I miss you like crazy, and I did not apologize to you the right way when we separated. My head is clear now, and I want to say that I am genuinely sorry for hurting you. I have been miserable without you, and I can't take it anymore. I want our friendship back. I want you. I can't do this life without you. Can you please find it in your heart to forgive me?"

"I already have. You hurt me, Zanny, but I am good, and you are forgiven, but I do not know about us being friends. I can't be your friend, and you know that."

"Why not? Ok, I understand that, but I am asking you to give me all of you. I do not want to just be friends. I know you are in a relationship……."

"O so that is what this is about? Because I am with someone? Wow, how shallow of you. You only want me because someone else has me, is that it? You do not want me; you want the likes of me. Why do men want to do right after he sees his ex with someone else? I can't believe you."

"No, Noel, this is not about you being with another man, well, not exactly."

"You see, right there. I am about to go." She got up to leave. I delicately grabbed her hand.

"Wait. Please just wait. Hear me out." She sat down slowly. I can tell she loved me but didn't trust me and I get it. I fucked up.

"I know you don't trust me, but I promise you that I have never forgiven myself for hurting you. I want what I had, and I will spend every day proving to you that I am worthy of your love and time. I am so sorry, Elly."

"Don't call me that. You know what that means to me. So, stop it."

"You called me, Zanny."

"I didn't realize it. I apologize."

"No apology needed." We sat and looked each other in the eyes, and I can tell she was feeling everything I was saying, but something was holding her back for some reason. I can't put my finger on it. So, I broke the silence.

"Can you see yourself giving me a second chance? Baby, please. I'll leave anyone alone who I am talking to. You can even sit there while I make the call. I don't care. All I care about is you."

"I am engaged."

BOOM!!!!!!!

That was what I couldn't put my got damn finger on. I knew something didn't feel right. What?????

"You're what? When? How?" I started to choke on my heart. I am so stupid! Of course, any man would see that she is a jewel.

"It's been a week now. And Zanny, I mean, Zander, he got down on his knee and asked me. That's how."

I finally looked at her left hand and noticed the ring!!! She has on a fucking ring!

I just looked at her and I couldn't move. I just couldn't. My world is ending. I fucked up. She's leaving me for another man. I can't take this. My chest is getting tight or is that my heart leaving my body. It doesn't matter. I'm starting not to feel so good.

"Zanny, are you ok?"

I just stared at my future wife, the mother of my children, the woman I would do anything for, and I wanted to die. Someone is taking her away from me. If I would have left my cheating ways alone, she would be mines. I'm so fucking selfish! Holy shit, I can't breathe!

"Someone call 911!"

Those were the last words that I heard before everything went black. I guess it's true with what they say, you can die from a broken heart.

Chapter 12

ZANIYAH ROZE ROYSS

RING

My phone kept ringing while I was in my last class of the day. My dance teacher was just in the middle of a pirouette, one of the most difficult ballet moves. I heard someone burst through the doors and used their hands to fan my instructor to walk over to them.

"Zaniyah, grab your things and go with this young lady."

"Who? Me?"

"Come now, Zaniyah, no games. Chop chop."

I grabbed my bags and went in the direction of the dressing room.

"No! Zaniyah, let's go. You can keep what you have on. Come now."

My mother doesn't even talk to me like that, but I listen when my dance instructor talks.

"Yes, Ma'am."

I grabbed my things and jogged over to the young lady.

"What the hell is going on?"

"I do not know, but you are excused for the rest of the day. Here is a note saying to get to Tampa General right away."

"Who is in the hospital?"

"I don't know, but it sounded urgent."

"Ok, thank you."

I panicked and ran to my car. My mother? I know I don't like her ass, but I love that woman. Who am I supposed to talk to when I get married or if I can't decide on whether to marry a man or woman! Who the hell can I talk to?

O my God! My father? He is older, but he is in the best shape of his life. How can that be? If it's him, I am going to just lay in the bed and die right alongside with him.

I got to the hospital quickly. I was only driving on two wheels.

"Hello, ma'am. Are you here for the Roze Royss family?" the receptionist asks me.

Well, hot damn. I love being rich.

"Yes, I am."

"Ok, come this way, please."

I was such in a rush to get there that I found myself on top of her heels. Why is this bitch walking so damn slow? She took me down a hall to an elevator that I assumed was for the rich and famous.

"Do you know what is going on? Who is in the hospital?"

"I am sorry, Ma'am, but your mother said she would explain everything to you when you get here"

"It's my father, isn't it?" I whispered to the nurse.

The nurse just stayed quiet on the short ride to the destinated floor.

"Zaniyah, are you ok?" My mother yelled when she saw the look of dread on my face.

"Ma is dad, ok? I need to talk to him before something happens to him."

"Ok, baby girl, it's not your dad."

"Soooo, who is it?" What? Then who am I here for. Right at this moment, the rest of the family came around the corner and sat down in the chairs. I looked at everyone as they looked at me, and then I saw Noel. Hold up.

"Noel, what are you doing here? Hold on! Wait a minute! Is this about Jr? Ma?" I looked at my mother with pleading eyes to tell me that I was wrong.

"Yes, baby. It's your brother. But…."

I just started crying…

"What happened?" I am delirious right now.

"He will be fine, Zaniyah. Calm down, sweetheart. He had a panic attack. After you calm down, you can go in to see him, but you must calm down, baby, ok?"

It took me a few minutes. I don't know much about the medical world, but I do know that a panic attack can kill you.

"Mom, I'm ready."

I went into the room, and all these wires and plugs were everywhere. He did not look like he was going to be ok.

"Hey, sis. You better wipe them tears." He said weakly, from his bed.

"I'll leave you two alone. Are you ok, Zaniyah?" My mother said kindly. I am surprised at how she is treating me. So soft, so tender.

"Yes, Ma'am."

I just looked at my brother for a moment to relish in the fact that he is still alive.

"Was your panic attack bad? Are you going to be, ok? You know you are my favorite."

He laughed.

My brother told me everything that led up to the attack. I was piiiiiiissed.

"Sis do not do anything to her. I plan on making her my wife."

"Even though she is getting married?"

"Yes. She is not married yet. The panic attack might have scared her enough that she doesn't want to lose me for real. At least, I hope so after all of this. I love that woman, Sis."

I am looking at my brother like he has lost his damn mind. But I guess love will do it to you.

"Does the family know what led to the attack?"

"Only you and Zada. So don't tell nobody else do you hear me?"

"I got you. I am just so glad that you are ok."

"No doubt Lil sis. I love you, big head."

"I love you too. When are you getting out?"

"Tonight. Noel is taking me home. So again, be nice."

"Will do."

I got up and kissed him on his forehead. I love this dude with his puck ass.

"Hey, can you tell mom and dad to come in here for me?"

"Sure. Stay sweet." I opened the door and told my parents they were being summoned. After they went into Jr's room, that was my cue.

"Noel, may I speak to you for a moment, please?"

"Sure."

We walked down the hall, and I directed her into an empty patient's room.

"Hey, Zaniyah. I am sorry about your……."

"I didn't pull you to the side to hear that. I pulled you to the side to say that my brother has never forgotten about you. He has always and will always continue to love you. He told me everything from the moment he cheated until this very second. So, I get why you are upset with him, however, I love my brother, and I will hurt a bitch over him. I understand you are taking him home tonight, but after you drop his black ass off, you need to decide if you want to be with him or not. With whatever decision you make, make it and stick to it. Don't string my brother along because obviously, you can see how he is affected by you. So, stay the hell away from my brother if you don't want to take him seriously. I am not trying to threaten you, but this is about my brother. That's all I have to say."

"Ok, I hear you, and I have already heard this from Zada as well. Did you two rehearse this or something? You know what, never mind that. I understand because if it was my brother, I would be overprotective too. I hear you, and I will decide. I already have, but I will sit on my decision a little bit longer. You and your sister are too cute. I love the bond you all have."

"Ok, Miss cute. Don't let the cuteness fool you. Let's get out of here before Jr thinks I am trying to kill you or something."

Chapter 13

ZANDELL ROZE ROYSS

Well, we are on our way home, and I am exhausted. I know my family tries to hide things, but I am not stupid. I was walking to the restroom and heard Zaniyah and Noel's whole conversation. My brother let a female send him over the top. That is insane; however, I am just happy that he is ok. He and I had a long talk, and he said the panic attack is making him reevaluate his life. He said how sorry he was for not being there for me and not being the role model, I need him to be.

He has me thinking about reevaluating my life as well. I am young, and I must stop taking things so seriously. I love basketball, but I also don't want to waste my childhood. I need to enjoy my youth just a little bit. So, I am going to enjoy myself at this party with my sister tomorrow. She will keep me busy, so I'll have to stay on her, but I am going to lay my hair down for the most part. I might just get a few numbers too.

We finally got home, and I am hitting the shower and going straight to bed. I have a big day tomorrow. I got to get fitted for this party, and I need to get a fresh cut. I'll have dad take me in the morning.

As I walked in the house, an unusual feeling fell on me, and I could not put my finger on it, but it felt like someone was watching me. I didn't know for sure, but I quickened my pace behind my parents and sister. This property is so big, and your mind starts to wonder. The family settled for the night, and I was ready to catch some z's for the big night tomorrow.

♣

"Good morning, champ. It's time to go and get that cut."

"Good morning, Dad. Ok, let me throw something on. I'll be down in a sec."

"Cool."

Today should be an easy, fun day. All my friends will be at the party tonight, and the females will be there too. I am banking on getting at least one person's number which shouldn't be that hard because all the girls are on me. But there is one person that I have been feeling for a minute, RayShonna. I think tonight is the night that I will be asking her out on a date. Hopefully, she says yes. I brushed my teeth, put on my high school hoodie, sweatpants, and air force ones. I ran down the stairs, and I saw my brother chilling in the family room.

"Hey, what's up bro. How are you feeling?"

"Oh, I am feeling great. I am here to take you to get a haircut for this party you're going to."

"What? I thought dad was taking me."

"Naw Lil homie. I'm taking you. We need to talk anyway. Are you cool with that?"

Lil homie? Huh? My brother does not talk like this. Smh

"That's perfect!"

We hit the road in my brother's all-black 2022 S-Class Mercedes-Benz with the butterscotch seats. He played the number one hit song, "Playboy" by Ca$h. We both had our caps on backward. I never had so much fun with my brother before. I hate to say it, but I am happy that he had something happen to him to wake up and value his family. I needed someone to talk to besides my dad.

"Hey, I wanted to get away from Bay Shore for a while. So, we are going to a barbershop in St. Pete. One of my homeboys opened a chain of shops, and I would like to support him. Cool?"

"Cool." I had the biggest grin on my face.

"So, let us talk. Do you have a girlfriend yet?"

"No."

"Why not? I know all the girls be on yo jock."

Man, my brother, talking like this is so cool. I'm loving this.

"There is this one girl I really like. Her name is RayShonna, but I am trying to focus on school. I don't want my grades to slip; I really want a college scholarship. I don't want pops trying to control me by paying for school. If I get a scholarship, it's taken care of. I have to do my part to keep it."

"Man, I wish I had brains like you when I was going up. You sound like you have it all mapped out. However, I love how you are taking care of your business, but I want you to have fun too. That doesn't mean get a girl pregnant anytime soon, though. You feel me?"

I laughed and nodded. "Yeah, I feel you."

"Have you had sex yet?"

"Yes."

"What do you mean yes? What did you do?"

"I put my thing in her, and she said it hurt so, I took my time because we were both virgins. And after about two minutes, I came."

"Two minutes? That's way too fast. You must control your mind. It's ok, you're young. You'll get the hang of it. Hahaha. Did you use protection?"

"Yes, I did."

"Good, never go without protection. Was it RayShonna?"

"No, it was some girl at a party. We played a truth or dare game."

"Wow, the young girls today. Be careful sleeping with random broads, though. They can have an STD. Make sure that you at least care for the girl. Don't be like me and have multiple chicks, and close out your heart. You'll find yourself losing a good girl."

"Are you talking about Noel?"

"Yes, I am. But I guess with what happened to me; she's decided to break off her engagement. So, we are seeing each other again. I'm cutting off every chick I am talking to. I will not mess this up."

"Congrats, Bro! That's what's up."

"Ok, we are here."

Jr parked right up front, and we got out of the car. When he locked the doors and started to walk, he stopped and turned to me.

"I want you to know something before we go in, and I mean this. I love you, Zandell. You can come and talk to me whenever you want or about anything, okay? Whether it's about guys, girls, life, maybe something you did or some type of way you may be feeling about something. I am serious with what I am saying. The first thing I said I was going to work on is our relationship. I will not see you fall by the waste side, and I will be here for you. You do not just have dad. You have me too."

And he gave me a tight brotherly hug.

"I love you too, Bro."

We walked into the barbershop and spoke to everyone. My brother started talking to his friend, and I was seated immediately. I shook the guy's hand, he and my brother started talking about old times. I just sat there thinking about the sex story I told my brother. I wanted to tell him that I didn't like having sex with the girl. It was the first and last time. My family thinks that I am a virgin, but I feel it's nobody's business but mines. And who cares what anyone thinks.

RING

"What's up, Alex."

"Hey Zandell, are you still going to the party tonight?"

"Yes, I am. You?"

"Definitely. Are you still bringing your sister? I don't feel like watching her fast ass. I'm trying to get my own swerve on."

"Don't sweat it. I'll make sure she's good. You don't have to keep tabs on her."

"O yeah, I took some Hennessy from my dad's cabinet. Are you going to take some shots with me?"

"I will. I'm going to ask my brother if he can drop us off and pick us up. His new ride is where it's at. We can bump that new Ca$h song, I just heard it. He is awesome."

"Bet."

My brother was wrapping it up with his friend, and I saw my father walk in. But he looked different. He had on a USF windbreaker pants set and a USF cap. My father never dresses like that. My dad was fitted to the nines. He sat in a chair; it looked like he just came to chat it up with the fellas. My brother was running his mouth and didn't even notice that Dad was here. Something was off about him. The way he talked and handled himself was not like him.

"Hey, Dad. What's up with the gear? I like it."

"I'm sorry. You have the wrong person."

"Ha-ha, Dad stop playing."

"No, I'm serious, son, you must be mistaken." He looked at me and seemed frightened like I was a ghost.

"Hey Zandell, is there a problem?" My brother started walking over. "Dad? What are you doing here? If I had known you was coming, you could have ridden with us."

"Listen, I am so sorry, but I am not your dad. You got the wrong person. Hey, I'll catch up with yawl later. I'm out." He got up and walked out of the shop. My brother and I looked at each other like we each grew a third eye. My brother went after our so-called father, and I followed right behind him. Jr finally caught up with him and grabbed his arm. My dad pulled away from him.

"Dad, what is wrong with you?"

"I am not your father."

"Ok, please explain to me why you're trippin? You are Zander Roze Royss Sr, right? You must be joking or something."

All the color on my dad's face left his body, and he is as brown as they come. So, you know something was not right.

"No, that is not my name. That's my twin brother. My name is Zain Roze Royss. I haven't seen my brother in years."

Our mouths dropped open.

Chapter 14

Zander Roze Royss Jr

"Wait a minute, wait a minute, wait a minute. I don't understand. My father never told us about a twin brother. You have to be our dad, or I am losing my mind. I just had a panic attack, so give me a minute to catch my breath."

"It's a long story. I shouldn't even be talking to you, fellas. I promised your dad I wouldn't be involved in your lives. If I would have realized you were in the shop, I would have left before you saw me. I just haven't seen pictures of you all in a while. This is bad. I can't talk to yawl. Just forget that you ever saw me."

"How are we supposed to do that? No. We are going to take care of this today. Do you live close by?"

"I do. I live on North Shore. Why?"

"Because we can go and get you an overnight bag. You are coming with us. We are straightening this out tonight."

"Look, young man. Don't stand here and talk to me like that. You don't tell me what to do. Now, this is over." He turned to walk away, and I grabbed his arm again.

"Look, I don't mean to sound pushy. But we have never heard of you. We want to know why. You are our uncle, and you are family. We were raised to take care of our own, and if my father cast you out, turned his back on you, or anything like that, I have a problem with him. I just want to know what is going on and get the truth for once. Do you have a family? A wife and kids?"

"I do not."

"Ok, well, you have a helluva lot of nieces, nephews, and a great-niece. So, what do you say?"

"There is a lot you don't know and might not understand. I really don't like this."

"I am grown. I can deal with anything that comes my way. We can handle it."

I can tell that this was too much for my Lil bro.

"Zandell, are you ok?"

"Yes and no. I just can't believe Dad lied to us."

"Well, Dad didn't lie, he just hid important information from us. Ok, so are you coming with us tonight, Zain? I mean Uncle, I guess."

"Sure, since you are not going to let this go."

"Nope. And I'm a lawyer."

"Figures. I should have known."

"Zandell, do you still want to get dropped off at the party?"

"Naw, I want to stay home and see what this is all about. This seems to be more interesting than the party."

"I hear that."

We followed my uncle in his red Porsche' to a high rise in St. Pete right off the water. We have land, but my uncle is by himself, so he owns a condominium, and it looks rich, smells rich and probably tastes rich. Go ahead with your bad self-Uncle. We waited in his condo for him to get an overnight bag. We are all staying in the main house tonight. I called my sisters and told them all to come over for an important family meeting.

"Uncle Zane, what do you do for a living?"

"Your father and I own Roze Royss realty. We have a few chains, and I run the one in St Pete. Roze Royss Realty is huge. We are all over the world, our company is very lucrative, and you all are lucky to be a part of a fortune five-hundred-dollar company. We are big. Your dad probably never told yawl that. He is selfish."

"Wow. I am speechless. And you sure is right about that." Damn daddy. That man is so cruel.

His place is amazing. The condo had the latest upgrades with marble floors with an exquisite double-door foyer. There were huge doors all throughout with wooden flooring. The kitchen had granite countertops with an island. There was an ocean view from one wall to the other, with a balcony. My uncle has great taste. While we sat in the family room, looking at the ocean view, a woman came from the bedroom with a silk robe on in heeled slippers with fur on the top. She only had on panties and bra underneath the somewhat see-through robe. She didn't give a damn that we were there. I have a fifteen-year-old brother sitting here for goodness' sake, and he's about to drool. I just let him look because I couldn't take my eyes off her myself. She was brown skin and tall, about 5'9. She had light brown eyes and looked like a model. I know I seen her somewhere before. My Uncle came out of the room oblivious to his half-way naked girlfriend.

"Hey, guys, this is Tiffany. She wanted to meet you. She never met my family before other than my brother. These are my nephews Zander Jr and Zandell. I'll be back. Let me grab a few more things. Tiff will keep you company. Sorry about her attire, she hates clothes. Yawl good?"

My brother and I was in a daze, "Yeah."

"Ok. Cool. Make them something to drink, Tiff." He yelled out as he walked away.

"Hello fellas, do you want something to drink? For Jr, I have something strong, and for Zandell, I have some soda. Is that ok?"

We were mesmerized. Wow.

"Umm, no, thank you. I'm good." I tapped Zandell with my elbow for him to say the same, but this lil horny boy didn't.

"Yes, do you have Gatorade? I'm an athlete."

Really Zandell!!! Really. Did you have to throw athlete in there?

"Ok. I'm on it." She's sexy and her voice sounds like roses.

We had our drinks and talked to her for a moment. My Uncle was finally ready. Thank goodness, I was getting hot as hell. I had to get out of there.

"Uncle, do you want to just ride with me? I can always bring you home."

"Thanks, Nephew. That's cool. I really appreciate that."

"Ok. Cool."

"It's nice to meet you, Tiffany." I shook her hand. Sooooo soft. My goofy behind brother did too. I wanted to laugh because he obviously had a woody.

When we walked out of the high rise, I had to ask.

"Is that your girl? Are you trying to marry that?"

"Hahaha no nephew. I have always had love for one woman, and if I can ever get her back, that's who I plan on marrying. Tiffany is just a friend with benefits."

"Ok, Got you. Who is this woman you are in love with?"

"I'd rather not say, but you will know when you see us in a room together. It's like magic."

"Go ahead Uncle Zane. Zandell, are you good?"

"Yes, I am. I am just waiting for when we get home. Are you going to call Dad and give him a heads up about all this?"

"Nope. I'm going to surprise him just like he surprised us."

I told my sisters there will be some drama at the house tonight so they can't miss it. They love drama when they are not the cause of it. This is a mess. I can't wait to hear the long story behind this cover-up.

We finally got to the estate; all the cars were parked outside, letting me know everyone was here. I was ready to get this party started. We walked in, and everyone was seated in the family room. Our maid stared at the man who looked like my father. She just pointed toward the family room door. She watched in disbelief. Zandell walked in the room first, then I, and finally the man of the hour, Uncle Zain. My father stood up out of his chair, bewildered.

"What in the hell are you doing here?"

"Long time no see, bro."

The look on my father's face was priceless. The moment my mother walked into the room; the energy changed; it was so weird. Everyone looked from my uncle to my mother. The room was quiet and still, and then it hit me like a ton of bricks. That knowing-of-true-love-look. Wooooooo! What a minute!

"Unc, is this the magic you were talking about?"

Ashamed, he looked away from my mother and at me. He didn't say a word, but the shit was written all over his fuckin face. Why is so much shit trying to make me lay in a coffin before my damn time?

Chapter 15

ZIOLA ROZE ROYSS

My body felt so good. Sr hadn't been home at all, and I didn't bother asking why. I hadn't felt this exhilarated since I don't know when. I saw the light for the first time since having my last child. My marriage with Zander started to dissipate after our last baby. He became so mean and angry all the time. He took it out on the first person who was closest to him, me. But this feeling I was feeling now was like the feeling I had when I first met my husband in college. My first love, my first true friend, my everything. Why am I feeling this way now? Standing before his brother. Jr started yelling and snapped me out of my trace.

"Can somebody tell me what the hell is going on? Why do you have a twin brother dad that we don't know about? You have a chain of companies that we don't know about. I knew we was rich, but you never explain we were filthy rich. Can someone explain?"

Zander Sr

"Zain, can I talk to you privately, please."

Zander Jr

"O no! It seems that we have been talking privately enough. Why did we not know about your twin brother, our uncle!"

All my children looked so lost. Their father lied to them and me. I knew he had a twin brother, but he told me that they had a bad falling out, and they do not talk anymore. So, I stopped bringing it up after my third baby.

Zander Jr

"Uncle Zain, I just met you today, but you have been the most honest person in this room, especially compared to my father." He stared Zander Sr down. "Can you tell me what this is all about?"

Zander Sr

"Ok. Enough is enough. I won't have it. Zain, get out of my house!"

Zander Jr

"Nope, he stays here. In fact, he's staying with me tonight, so I can hear the whole story. Go ahead, Unc, you have the floor."

Uncle Zain

He cleared his throat, hesitating for a moment.

"I hope that I don't make anyone feel uncomfortable, but I may. Ziola, this story is all about you. I know it will sound weird but believe me, it is true. Please have a seat by Jr."

I looked at Zander Sr, and his eyes forbid me to do it, but my kids were here, and I knew he couldn't do anything to me. Plus, I wanted to hear this. So, I walked over to the chair and sat by Zander Jr, who was standing up.

Uncle Zain

"Ok. Ziola, I met you when we were going to the University of South Florida. It was our senior year right before graduation. I was on the fence with my grades knowing that I would not graduate if I did not get it together. I didn't have time to date, but you did something to me, and I did not want to lose you. So, I thought up a plan in which my brother and I have done a thousand times. I asked him to be me and date you for me. Only until graduation." He looked over at my dad and got nothing. So, he continued.

"After graduation, everything moved fast. With us opening the real estate company and getting it up and running, I didn't have time to take you out. I took the business way more seriously than Zander, so my focus was different than his. I begged him to continue with this charade. Through the talks that you two had, my brother told me you wanted children, and that would be a deal-breaker for you if your man couldn't give you that. You never knew this, but I have always been baron. I still got checked by a friend of my in the medical field just to be sure, and they confirmed it. I loved you so much and wanted you to have what you desired, that I talked my brother into giving you the life you've always wanted, marriage, kids and love. Since I couldn't give you what you needed, my brother agreed and promised to take care of you. It hurt me too bad to stick around and watch, so I left. I am so sorry, Ziola, but I promise you that I only wanted you to be happy. It killed me to let you go."

I wanted to slap the shit out of him! I lived a whole fake life. You wouldn't believe it, but they were identical, and I truly could not tell the difference between the two. So, it was very easy for them to pull this off. I did start to feel a little different, but I honestly did not know why. No wonder I was getting fucked up! Because I had a man that didn't love me at all. He just did his brother a favor.

"So let me get this right. I have been living a lie? I am married to a man who does not love me and never did? He just gave me children? So, you took away my option whether to live with that or not? How dare you make that decision for me. And you!!" I looked Zander Sr square in the eyes. "You will pay for all of what you put me through and for all of what you have done to me."

I got up and looked at everyone, including the ex-love of my life and then diverted my attention to the thorn-in-my-ass-of-a-fucking-husband. I usually don't get hood, but when the time is right, what can I do?

"So, you wanna play games with people's lives?" Zander started shaking his head no. He feared what might come out of my mouth. But don't worry dear, I won't let everything out of the bag yet. My kids were looking crazy because they'd never heard me as much as yell.

"You got some fucking nerve. You played me like a yo-yo. I have been your pawn for years." I was slowing and dangerously walking closer to him as I spoke until I was up in his grill. "To think that I did something wrong to make you hate me so much when I know I did nothing wrong but love you. You made me feel disgusted all these years. You selfish piece of shit."

"Now hold on, Ziola, I am…"

"Shut the fuck up! I am talking now! It's my turn." Zander closed his mouth and let me have the floor.

"I loved you, I cooked for you, washed your funky ass suits, I sexed you how you wanted to be sexed, and I won't go into further detail on that shit, I gave you my hand in marriage, I had your babies, and I raised them according to your stupid ass rules, you arrogant bastard. I made you feel like a king when I knew you were lower than hell, I lovingly educated yo ass when you didn't know shit, and I helped you with this palace of ours. And the payback that I get is you lying to me by helping your coward ass brother not to be a man and handle his business in telling the woman that he loves that his ass is fucking baron?" She looked over at Zain swiftly. "Oh and Zain, you ain't off the hook, homeboy, but I'll get with you later, but for right now, I need to deal with this piece of rat shit right here." I looked back at my filth of a husband while all the kids' eyes were glued on me and speechless.

"This is why you treated me like you did. You didn't love me. You were forced to deal with me. So now it all makes sense. Your love is not with me, and that is why you have another whole fucking family! Yes, kids, your father has a woman with three kids who are triplets and another one on the way!"

Zander Jr

"What the hell!"

Zandell

"Dad?"

Zaniyah

"Wow."

Zada

"I can't fucking believe this."

Zandra

"What else can go wrong tonight! I hope I have a sister, though."

"Shut up, Zandra. Not now!" I snapped.

"Yes, Ma'am."

"And to think I gave you my all. Now it's time for you to sit your ass there and talk to your kids about their long-lost family. Oh, and by the way, I invited your other family to Sunday dinner tomorrow. We are a family after all, right?"

Sr stood up and got in my face.

"What the fuck?" He snarled.

And I raised my voice to another whole octave that he wasn't used to hearing. I shocked myself too.

"What the fuck? What the fuck? Sit yo ass down, Zan. You ain't going to do shit but lay in the fucking bed you made. So, get out of my got damn face!" Zander looked at me for a second and sat back down. He knew I was right.

"I am going to turn in for tonight due to a very big day tomorrow. Sr Dear, if you so much as try to come into MY bedroom tonight, I will shoot you and kill you. Goodnight, all. I guess I'll see everyone in the morning. Zandra and Zandell, come with me to my room, please. Your older siblings can handle yo raggedy-ass daddy however they please."

And I walked my pretty ass out of the room along with my babies in tow. I have never felt so low and alive at once, in my life before this very moment. I was a bit sad, but I mainly felt free. Finally, I would be getting a divorce and walking away with my babies and a shit load of money.

Chapter 16

Zada Roze Royss

Everyone started shouting at my father. I couldn't believe all the shit that went down in this house tonight. My family is officially crazy, dysfunctional, and delusional. My brother, Jr, was now up in my father's face, wanting to beat his stupid ass. My little brother and now new uncle were trying to hold these two damn fools apart.

Zander Jr

"How could you, dad? You fucked this whole family up with your controlling ways. And the way my mother was talking, it seemed like you physically hurt her too. If I find out that you hurt my mother, you won't have to worry about her shooting and killing you because I'm going to do it for her."

Zain

"Ok, everyone, just calm down."

Zander Sr

"This is all on you." My father charged at him.

It was a mess. Nothing got discussed because everybody was hurt and yelling.

Zain yelled over everyone. "Everybody come on, we need to talk about this!" The fight got broken up finally, and everyone backed up into their own corners.

It was finally calm enough for me to speak. "Dad, who do you have kids with? What other life is mom talking about?"

"Ok, everything your uncle said was right. I agreed to take care of your mother. I am so sorry that I did it, but my brother and I did everything for each other back then and so, I did this horrible thing. However, I had a love in my life that I found much later, and I couldn't get it out of my head how I could have had her instead of my brother's woman. I fell for the girl hard but of course; I couldn't marry her. This is hard to talk about."

"No, dad. Go on. You have left us in the dark for too long. Stop hiding and come out with it. The deed is done, so let's finish this. Tell us, please. We deserve to know. What's her name, what does she do, how many kids do you two have…"

"Ok. Umm, I met a woman named, Beverly."

Zandra

"Beverly? Dad, is this the woman you took me to to get my hair done?"

"Yes, baby girl."

Zandra

"Really, Dad?"

Zander Sr

"Again, I am sorry about this. Maybe Zandra and Zandell shouldn't be in here for this."

With a look of disgust and anger, I let my dad have it. "It's a little too late for that. We are mature enough to handle this. Zandra, sit your ass back down and let dad finish." Zandell went to sit by his baby sister and put his arm around her.

I smiled at my baby brother becoming a man and protector.

With calmness and poise, Zandell spoke.

"Ok, dad, you have the floor again. Continue."

"Well, yes, you are correct, Zandra, it is the same woman. There was just something about her. Next thing you know, we are in a full-blown relationship."

"Do she know about mom?" I ask.

"At first, no, but I told her after a while and explained the whole story to her. She was upset at first, but she continued seeing me and then she got pregnant. She had triplets. Two boys and a girl."

"Wow, dad. This should be on reality TV. How old are they?"

"They are sixteen."

Zandell

"A year older than me. You have been messing with this woman for a long time, Dad."

"I know, son. I have. The kids did not know about any of this until about a week ago. Everything happened so fast, and I haven't been able to wrap my head around it."

I shook my head. "Mom mentioned that this Beverly woman is pregnant again. Is she correct?"

"Yes, it is. She is five months pregnant. I am so sorry, you guys."

Everyone fell silent, probably from everyone's blood pressure hitting through the roof earlier. With so much going on right now, I just wanted to go to sleep. I was supposed to meet Raphael tonight, but I really wasn't feeling it. We heard the door open, and everyone looked toward the entrance. It was my stupid ass husband and my beautiful daughter.

"Hello, everyone. What's been happening? Did I miss something?" He looked around the room, and as he made it around to the left side, his facial expression changed, looking between my uncle and my dad. "Wow, there is two of you?"

He makes me so sick, just look at hm. Looking like a dumbass deer in front of some bright-ass headlights. I rolled my eyes at my husband as he looked at my uncle.

"Uncle Zain, do you have somewhere to stay tonight? You are welcome to come to my home with my family and me."

"Awww thanks, niece, but I am staying with Zander Jr."

Zander Sr

"With my son? You're not going back home?"

Zain

"No, I am not. Plus, Ziola said for everyone to be here for dinner tomorrow, and I wouldn't miss it for the world. Also, I need to talk to my nephew. Seems like I have catching up to do with all of you, but I can start with Jr."

Zaniyah finally spoke.

"I am staying with you guys tonight too. I want to catch up with you, and I need a drink. My head hurts from all this BS."

Zandell

"I'm going to Jr's house too. Is that ok, Jr?"

Zander Jr

"It sure is. Whoever wants to catch up, let's go."

"Do you want to go, Zandra?"

Zandra

"Yup."

Zander Sr

"So, everyone is going to leave?"

Everyone said in unison.

"Yup"

I sighed. "Good night, dad. We will see you tomorrow at dinner. Remember to leave mom alone. I surely do not want to go to a funeral right after all this mess."

Everybody started laughing. I guess we are in an ok place because our home always felt out of place, really. It's funny, but Zain should have been our dad. The way he carried himself suited us more than what we had with our biological father. He was laid back and simply just cool. My dad has always been uptight, and now I know why. This is not where he wanted to be.

Everyone got in their rides and went to my brother's property. When I got home, I got my baby girl into bed for the night and went to grab something quick to eat. As I was about to make my mayo, mustard, ham and cheese sandwich, my fool-of-a-husband walked in.

"Can you make me one as well?"

I laughed at his damn nerve. "No, you can make your own."

"How did I know you would say that? That's why I threw away the mayonnaise and mustard. Hahaha." And the bastard walked out of the kitchen.

I looked in the frig and damn sho nuff. No damn mayo or mustard. That son of bitch! I calmed down and made peanut butter and jelly sandwiches. Now ain't that a bitch.

PHONE BEEPS

Dammit. I saw 30 missed calls and 15 text messages. Raphael!

Text messages

Hey, Red, I wanted to see if you can get out tonight.

Red, what's good?

Red, are you busy, if so, I'll holla at you another time.

Red, what is going on? I've been calling you.

Red, don't ignore me like this, you know that I will pull up.

Red just text me that you ok. It's been 3 hours.

Red enough is enough, I'm coming by. You about to have a nigga call these damn hospitals in a minute. I hate that you got me sweating you like this, Red. This ain't right. Be by in a minute.

Damn, I see you are wit the fam. Ok. I texted, and you didn't answer, so your phone might be put away. My bad. Text me when you can. And no, I wasn't stalking you. I just don't like to worry. Enjoy your night. O yeah and I saw yo boy getting mighty cozy with a chick today too. You need to leave that nigga. I'm out.

Look, I know my husband flirt, and honestly, I don't care. I would love to catch him cheating so I can have a reason to bounce even quicker. So, I went ahead and texted him back.

Hey babe, I am sooo sorry I messed your calls and texts. Thanks for checking up on me. It feels good to know somebody cares. I love you, and I will text you when I wake up in the morning. I am exhausted. Kisses.

I went to my room and washed up then lied down. I was mentally and physically drained, but before I could fall asleep, my stomach churned and I jumped up, sprinting to the bathroom. I empty my stomach out, feeling a little dizzy. What the fuck this bastard did to my sandwich! He's trying to poison me and shit. I crawled back into bed and closed my eyes, slowly counting to one hundred to sleep away these cramps.

When the sun was shining into my room, I jolted out of sleep at the sound of banging on the door.

"Zada, get up. I got to go somewhere!"

"Mommy." I heard my daughter on the other side of the door. She's two and is the best thing that this relationship created.

Damn, it's the morning already. At least I feel a little bit better. I don't know what the hell that was last night, but I bet I know who did it. I got up to unlock my door and took my daughter from my stupid husband's arms. He walked away and left immediately without a word. I went downstairs to get me some freshly cut canned pineapples and put them on a plate. And yes, I said canned pineapples. I don't trust that muthafucka. When I got back to my room, my daughter and I watched her cartoons on the tube. Suddenly, my stomach started acting up, and my mouth got watery again. What the fuck!! I jumped up and went to the bathroom, turned on the faucet and kept the door cracked to keep an eye on my daughter. I washed my face and brushed my teeth. Dammit man. I must still have that poison left in my system. Oh, I hate him. I got back in bed and started to resume watching TV with Alexis.

It just hit me! HOLY SHIT!!! When was the last time my period came on! I grabbed my phone and my app showed two weeks late. But that can't be. I am on birth control. Wait! I missed a few pills last month when I switched purses because of partying with Raphael's ass. OOOOOHHHHHH MYYYYYY GOODNESS! Raphael! Pregnant! No, just calm down, Zada. My nerves got so bad, I started to pace the room. Fuck, Fuck, Fuck!

"Hey, love bunny, we have to take a ride to the store, ok? Mommy is going to put your slippers on."

"Ok, Mommy!"

As soon as we left my room, I ran to the bathroom again and threw up once more.

My daughter and I went to Walgreens to grab a pregnancy test. As soon as we got back home, I ran to my room to take it. My daughter laughed at how I was acting crazy and running around like a headless chicken. I whipped out the stick, I peed on it and sat there staring. I heard the doorbell. Damn. I put the stick in the cabinet under the sink. I grabbed Alexis and went to get the door. It was my siblings and Uncle with breakfast. I was the only one not present at my brother's house last night, so I guess they all wanted to come by here to include me.

"Hey, everyone come on in. Wow, food." My stomach was turning at the sight of it.

"Zaniyah, take everyone to the kitchen. I'll be right back. Hi mother."

"No, no, no. None of that, do not call me mother again. Your father thought that was the proper thing to say. I've always hated that. Mom or ma is fine, love."

Wow, go, mom!

"Ok, mom it is. I'll be right back."

I kissed her on the cheek, and she took Alexis from me. I ran up the stairs, went back into the bathroom and grabbed the stick. I was nervous about opening my eyes, and with them still closed, I heard,

"HOLY SHIT, congrats Sis!" My eyes shot open. Zaniyah standing in the doorway, with that beautiful college youth glow, smiling.

Chapter 17

ZANIYAH ROZE ROYSS

My sister looked at me like she saw a ghost. It looked like she was in shock.

"Zada are you ok. Do I need to call 911?"

"No, don't. What are you doing up here?"

"I wanted to come and check on you. Is that a bad thing? Did you sleep in this guest room last night? I am a bit confused. Why do I feel like another situation is going on that I don't know about? What's up, sis?"

Out of the blue, she started crying. What the fuck is up with my family?

"Sis, what's wrong? Hold up. Come out of here and sit on the bed." I shut and locked the bedroom door.

"What is going on? Talk to me." I wiped her tears and rubbed her back. She slowly calmed down. I have never seen my sister not have it together before.

"I'm sorry to have cried like that in front of you."

"It's ok. You're not happy that you're having a baby?"

"Yes, I am very happy. I am just not ready for no one to know. Especially you."

"Why not me?"

"You are always looking up to me, and this is a sticky situation. If you have never kept a secret before, you must keep this one."

"You know I'm down for whatever. Period. I love you, and I am not going anywhere. So, lay it on me. What's up?" I was dead ass serious. This is my damn sister at the end of the day.

"I need to start from the beginning so that you will understand. The family does not know this yet, but Alex and I haven't been on the best of terms for the past two and a half years. It seems like when he found out I was having a girl instead of a boy, he just changed. He didn't want to touch me, talk to me, nothing. After I had my daughter, I was home, on leave, taking care of the baby, and I found out he was cheating on me. I saw text messages on his phone, and you know I immediately addressed him about it. He told me to my face that he will be sleeping in the other room. He said I disgust him. I was so hurt and disappointed. He started hitting the streets, and I knew he was with someone. One time I even found panties in his pocket. That was the last straw, so I told him I wanted a divorce, and he threatened to take me to the cleaners. We do not have a prenup, so I am stuck. I will get my divorce, but it will take time."

That muthafucka! I am trying to be calm, but I am fuming inside.

"Wow, Sis. And now you are pregnant with his child. Just give him half and call it a day. Dad will make something happen."

"Well, that's the thing."

"What? Has he been hitting you?"

"No. I haven't had sex with him in a year. We haven't touched each other."

Hold the fuck up!

"Sooooo who have you been messing with? Who is the father?"

"Raphael Lovechild aka Ca$h."

I almost passed out and died.

"What in the fuck! My quiet, loving, bashful ass sister is fucking an artist. And the number one top artist at that, and you didn't goddamn tell me! Holy shit! Zada, give Alex's ass whatever he wants, your double rich bitch!"

My sister and I started laughing and crying together.

"Ca$h like the Playboy Ca$h?"

"Yes. We have been seeing each other for over a year now. I have been having the time of my life. Going to his house parties, being on his arm. Everybody knows me. I love that man so much."

I can see it in her eyes that she truly means this.

"Wow, sis. This is deep. What do you think he will say?"

"He will be ecstatic. He doesn't have any kids yet. He has already told me to leave Alex, and I don't want to tell him about how Alex has been threatening me. I don't want to upset him. I want to try and handle this on my own. Especially now that I am pregnant, I must keep this on the hush. Today I am making an appointment with Jr to see if he can recommend someone to help me with my divorce. It's going to go down after my pregnancy is out."

"You do not have to worry about me saying anything. I will be here if you need me. Call me if he tries anything. Damn, I have to wear my poker face around that bastard. I am so sorry you are going through this, Sis." I hugged her. "I'm right here if you need me. Always. I love you."

"I love you too."

"Ok come on and let's get downs stairs before everybody start coming up here. Give me your pregnancy test. I'll trash it when I leave, you do not want to carry that around."

"Great idea." She passed me the test and I put it in my crossbody purse. We got up and headed for the stairs. When we started to descend, Alex walked his retarded ass in the house.

"Hey everybody. Wow did I miss something again?"

You damn sure did with your dumb ass. You damn sure did

Chapter 18

Ziola Roze Royss

My chef was in the kitchen cooking up a storm. You would think it was Thanksgiving up in here. I was in the best of moods because this marriage is basically over. I have not talked to my kids about the divorce yet, but I will. I have the dining room looking fabulous. I cannot wait to see his boo thang and his kids. Zander's genes are strong, so I am sure they look just like him. Hopefully, I don't break down and cry.

I am upset and will be getting a divorce; I thought the man I married was another man all along by how he treated me. I could not tell the difference because I had been dating them both since the beginning of time. However, they played me, but I will be laughing in the end. I can't believe that after I take half of what he has, his newfound family will still be financially straight. It's all good though, he can have the big house, and they can, too. I will build my own on the property in the far back and maybe have a second entrance, so no one will know what I am doing. That's right! I am not going nowhere.

I looked at my beautiful face as I started to apply my foundation. I hate make-up so much. I wear it because of my husband. Omg! You know what? What is wrong with me? I don't have to do a damn thing anymore. I am taking out this raggedy-bone-straight-ass-ponytail and these long ashy lashes. I have very long natural hair, and my own lashes are just as long and pretty. I am going to dinner as myself.

I stripped my body down of all my added additions. Then I jumped in the shower and washed my hair with a smile on my face. I was thinking about what I would wear. O yes! I had the perfect dress in mind. As I got dressed, I heard a knock at the door.

"Who is it?"

"Me, mommy."

My baby Zandra. I unlocked the door.

"Mom, you…"

"Ugly?"

"No, beautiful."

"Awwww, thank you, baby." I gave her the biggest hug.

"I am so serious, Mom. The family is going to flip when they see you. You know what? I am about to pick my hair out just like you. I'll be right back. We have 45 mins left." She ran off to her bathroom.

Wow, all I needed to do was just be a mother and be myself. I got a little emotional with the reaction my daughter gave.

The time struck 6:40 pm. I heard the dishes and the maids putting the dining room table together for our guests. I also heard

Zander Sr telling one of the maids that she needed to dust more. I have never seen him in a frenzy like I have seen today. He must really love this girl. He and I haven't been talking at all. He went to work one morning, and by the time he came back, I had all the maids put every one of his things in the spare bedroom. He wasn't sleeping in here with me. My enslavement days are over. He knew not to touch me again.

I heard the doorbell rang, and I am assuming that that's our guests for the evening. I told the maids for everyone to be in the family room until my daughter and I come down the stairs, and I will direct them to the dining room table myself. I reached for my daughter's hand, and she smiled. My daughter was dressed up with cut-up jeans, an all-white t-shirt with a black woman on the front along with the words, I Am a Black Nubian Goddess. She had on red all-stars, adorned with her red earrings to match the queen's headwrap on her shirt. My daughter looked so cool. Her father will have a heart attack because we are dressed out of the norm but good for us, fuck him.

As we descended the stairs, I heard my kids talk to this family that we are all ready to meet. Zandra walked through the doors first, and her sisters thought she was so cute with her high puffs tied high with her red wrap. But the looks that I got was the exact reaction that I knew would come. Again, I am the Queen of this castle and the crown on my head made it known.

I had on an orange African dress wrap with blue peacock feathers plastered all over. The dress straps laid to the left side over my shoulder. The chest part had an opening just enough to show a hint of beautiful, lifted cleavage. The high split on the left side of the dress went all the way up to my upper thigh. It showed off my light brown toned legs along with my diamond blue stuttered low heels. And to top everything off, I had on no makeup at all, just wet glittery gloss, no lashes, blue stuttered hoops, and my hair was picked out in an afro with a blue headband to push my afro slightly back.

"Mom, you look beautiful!" Zaniyah gasped.

Zaniyah walked up to me and kissed me on the cheek as well as my other children. I knew I was a showstopper.

Zander Sr

Zander walked up to me and stared into my eyes. I thought he would give me a tongue lashing, and I was ready to cuss his ass out in front of the old babies and the new ones.

"You look fabulous." What the fuck? Really? Now I know for sure, I am divorcing his ass. I could have been myself years ago. His mistress Beverly walked up to me with her triplets, and we greeted each other with our eyes at first.

"Hello Beverly, it's good to meet you." Beverly was attractive. She had glowing brown skin and pouty lips. Her eyes were slightly slanted like she is Asian, and she had shoulder-length hair that was blown out. She looked natural as well. Her glow came from the baby she was caring, I am sure. She had on a summer black maxi dress with sandals and her secondhand jewelry. However, the ring on her finger spoke Zander all day. Her kids were dressed to the nines. Her daughter had a half afro with the top in a puff and the back out. Very pretty young lady. The boys were spitting images of my sons.

"Hello Ziola, it's good to meet you too." Everyone was quiet and most likely scared to move. They didn't know how I was going to react. I moved to shake the children's hands.

"This must be Zahara. You are beyond beautiful. You look like your sisters."

Zahara replied, "Thank you. You're pretty too." She smiled, but I could tell she is nervous, sad, upset, and confused.

"Why, thank you, love." I moved to the next child. "Hello, and are you Zachary or Zanar?"

"I am Zachary, ma'am."

"Very handsome, both of you gentlemen are. You look just alike. Just like your father and his twin uncle."

"Twin Uncle?" All the kids said in unison, but the mother didn't look surprised. I fuckin bet. He most likely told her everything. Ass rabbit! You know how it goes. You're the wife and don't know shit, but the mistress knows every goddamn thing. Always got us looking stupid as hell. Zander is a damn crab. So, I moved to the third twin and put out my hand to shake it, but he did not reach back.

Zander and Beverly started in on him, but I spoke.

"No, it's ok. He has every right to be upset."

I looked into Zanar eyes with the kindness of a mother talking to her son. "Zanar, I understand that this is a shock to you. This is a bit too much, and I get it. Your father has kept everyone in the dark, so I can see how you are not comfortable with this. I'm not either." I giggled just a bit. "But this is something we cannot control, and we must deal with it. But however bad it may be, I will never turn away my family, and that's what you are. You have five other siblings who will support and love you until you feel better about the situation. So, you do not have to shake my hand. I am not mad with you at all." I smiled. "Are you hungry? I have collard greens, mac and cheese, and a juicy ham waiting for us." He looked like he wanted to cry, so I offered up the food. I feel sorry for these babies. Their father was living two lives. They had no idea, and it's not fair to them either. I couldn't tell Zanar this, but, honestly, I am happier than a Bitch! Fucking happy, to be exact. I will be dancing my way down the aisle in the damn courtroom. Three kids and one on the way? Infidelity? Hahahaha, can I say I'm Rich Bitch!!!!!

"Yes, Ma'am."

"Ok, well, let's eat." I turned around so everyone can follow me.

"Ms. Ziola?" I turned back around, and he held out his hand. "Nice to meet you."

"Well, it's nice to meet you too, Zanar. Let's eat some good ole soul food, and then together, we can whip yo daddy's ass." He laughed so hard.

The ice was all the way broken. I laughed with him. I put my arm around his waist, his arm went around my shoulders, and we started to walk to the dining room table together.

Chapter 19

Zandra Roze Royss

I am looking around the table at this mess of a family, but I love that there's a lot of us. I've always liked that we were a big family. The brady bunch got nothing on us. I am proud of my mom. She is taking all of this in like a champ. I know I am young, but I know that my mom feels like she has won the jackpot. I know she wants to jump ship, but she is still here because of us. My mother looks so beautiful tonight. I was looking at her presence and how strong she looks. I have not seen this side of her, ever. My brother Zandell was talking to the twins, and they were really vibing like true brothers. My sisters were talking to Beverly, my mom and dad. This was all so weird, and I am suddenly not feeling this. Why is everyone acting so normal? I can't take it no more.

"Why is everyone acting so normal like this is, ok? It is not ok!" I ran up the stairs to my room and slammed the door.

Ziola got up to go to her daughter. "I'll be back. Let me go and talk to her."

"Can I try Ms. Ziola?" Her brother Zanar asked.

"Sure."

"Do you want to come along, Zahara?"

"I thought you'd never ask." Zahara got up and followed her brother.

Ziola

"Her room is to the left when you get to the top. It says Danger Zone on the door."

"Ok." They giggled.

I heard footsteps and thought it was my mom coming. I just really didn't want to be bothered.

"I don't want to be bothered, mom."

"It's Zanar and Zahara."

I sat up. My new siblings came to talk to me. Wow. I wiped my tears with my pillow and put it down in front of me. I couldn't have them looking at me like I'm a big ass baby.

"You can come in." I couldn't believe they came up instead of my mom. They don't know me. Why are they here? Doesn't my door say Danger Zone muthafuckas? Even though my brother is 6 ft, and my sister is 5'7, I can hang with the best of them.

"Come in."

Zanar spoke.

"Hey, you."

Zahara spoke.

"Hi."

Zanar asked, "Are you ok?"

"Do I look ok? How are you guys ok with this? Dad did the ultimate betrayal to this family. Not to say you're not family but, you know what I mean. How are we supposed to be a family with how we became one?"

Zanar chimed in.

"We can't think about our parents and their shit. We can only think about ourselves and how to become tighter. We have to be there for each other."

Zahara added, "That's right. I am happy that I have a little sister. I am always around these boys, and it gets annoying because they are always trying to protect me. But to have a sister, someone I can protect or love, is pretty cool."

"Well, I can protect and take care of myself. I don't need it."

They started to laugh.

Zahara spoke.

"I believe you; you are a firecracker."

I smiled because I was glad, they recognized.

"I am still feeling some type of way."

Zahara spoke.

"I know what you are feeling."

"You don't understand my feelings," I said rudely.

"Yes, I do. Let me ask you something, do you feel like you will be replaced? That you will not be a daddy's little girl anymore?" Zahara asked.

I didn't understand my own feelings, so how will she know how I'm feeling? But my smart-ass sister hit it on the head.

"Zandra, it's ok to feel that way. I found out about you first. I saw your pink bookbag in the back of dad's car with the key chain that said daddy's little girl on it. And I was devastated to know that my dad had a daughter, a little girl. So, I immediately felt like I wasn't his pride and joy. I cried to my mom and yelled at him, but my mother told me something that I will tell you. She said that a parent's love is overflowing, it's grand, massive, and powerful. Parents have enough love to go around for everyone. That's why your mom is being so kind right now because she has that kind of love to offer too. It's a parent thing."

Wow, I couldn't have said that better.

"Wow, thanks, Zahara. That was powerful." I agreed.

"No problem."

Zanar chimed in.

"If it makes you feel any better, I punched Dad in the face when I found out about it?"

"What? You punched my daddy? I should beat your ass for that."

"Hey, I was mad too, but that's all that happened. Zachary and Zahara held us apart."

"Well, it makes me feel a little better because that's what I wanted to do when I found out. Tell me all about it. What did he do?"

I laughed at the story my brother and sister told me. Eventually, Zachary came in the room too when he heard our laughter. He felt it was safe at that point. Lol, I guess I have to get used to this. We all talked and really enjoyed each other's company.

Zahara said,

"Your house is so beautiful. I have never been in a mansion before. You're lucky. We have a super big house but not on a lot of land like you. My mom wanted to live in a neighborhood versus on land. But me, I'll take this house any day. Can I use your bathroom?"

"Sure."

We laughed and talked more about the incident with dad. I noticed how long she was in there. I hope she ain't shittin up my damn bathroom because I will call her on it. And she better not be stealing nothing either. Wait!!!!!

"Zahara, are you ok in there?" I said nervously.

"Ummm, Zandra! Come in here, please."

Hold shit balls!!! Did she see it!!!!

"Ok, here I come!"

Zanar giggled,

"Hahahaha, do you need a pad?"

Zachary added to the joke.

"Hahaha, or did you stop up the toilet?"

The boys were cracking up, but I found nothing funny at all. I walked up to the bathroom, and Zahara cracked the door to look at me.

"Yes," I whispered fearfully.

"Come in here please."

"Do you need a pad? If so, there are some under the sink."

"No, I don't need a pad, just come in."

I slid in the perfectly lavender, white and diamond bathroom fit for a princess like myself, and she began to unravel what I didn't want the world to know.

"Zandra, sit."

I sat on the toilet as I shook like a leaf, but I tried to remain as calm as possible.

"Yes?"

"What's this? And who's is it?"

I looked at the pregnancy test, and I started to cry. I put my face in my hands and sobbed.

"Shhhhhhh, I'm here. Oh Zandra, what are we going to do?"

"We, I'm the one it happened to. You can't tell nobody. I will handle this. Tell no one Zahara. Promise?"

"Zandra, we have to get help. You're thirteen. Did someone rape you? Were you molested?"

"No. It's my boyfriend's."

"Ok, well, at least it wasn't any type of assault. It will be ok. I will be quiet about this for now, but you must tell your mother or one of your sisters. They will help you through this. I'll be here for you too. Oh Zandra, why didn't you protect yourself?"

I shook my head. I'd been so damn stupid, that's why. "I don't know."

I continued to cry in my new sister's arms. Well, I guess we will be closer than ever now.

Chapter 20

Zander Roze Royss Jr

This whole week has been too much. A new uncle, new brothers and sister. I am overwhelmed with everything that is happening to my family right now. I am so glad that I have at least one thing in my life that makes me smile every day, two words. Noel Roland. I have the love of my life back in my life. How amazing is that? I know my family needs me, and I will be there every step of the way, but I have to live my life. Noel already went to work, now I need to get up and get my day started.

In the kitchen cooking my sausage, egg, and cheese McMuffin, my car alarm went off. I grabbed my keys and hit the button. I continued to cook my food, and my car alarm went off again. Damn, it's not raining nor windy. So, I hit the alarm again. Smh, I put the food on my plate, and the alarm sounded again. So, I decided to go outside to see what's going on. I walked out and saw some bull shit!

"What the fuck!!!!"

On my all-black Benz, someone spray painted "You Fuckin Whore" in white paint alongside the driver's side of the car. My breath caught up in my chest, and I had to take deep breaths to calm this panic attack that tried to come on. I immediately started looking around to see if I can see anyone on the property. There was no one. O my God! How am I supposed to get rid of this shit? My house!!! My door was open. I ran back into the house, and my breakfast was all over the kitchen counters, on the floors, and ketchup was on my white living room chairs. I started running through the house to see who in the hell was in here doing this. Then I heard the tires screeching out of the driveway. I ran to the door to see who it was. I saw a black 2021 Lexus speeding off my property. I knew exactly who it was.

RING!

"Hello."

"Lav, why the fuck did you mess up my car? And on my property at that?"

"I love you, Zander."

"O no, I broke off whatever we had a long time ago. So, what the fuck? I told you that our arrangement was over. I was honest with you about moving on with my life, and you were fine with that. This is not cool at all. I have a new life now, and I do not want you messing that up. You got the right one, I will ruin your life."

"Blah blah blah, you won't do shit, Zander! You thought that you could just walk away after three years of your punishing me with sex. I don't think so."

"Lavender, I am not playing. You ain't ready for this fight. Stay away from me."

"Nope, can't do. After you see what I put under your pillow, you'll see why you will always be a part of my life nigga!"

CLICK

Under my pillow, damn, her ass is fast. She went all up and through my damn house in minutes. I was scared to look under the pillow, thinking it might be a damn bomb. I quickly called my mechanic and asked him to fix my car. I called my office and told my secretary to hold all appointments this morning until I get in. I headed up the stairs and walked into the bedroom. I stared at the pillow like it was going to blow any minute. I snatched the pillow and jumped back. If you knew Lavender's history, you would be reacting the same way. It was a letter, and it read...

Dear Zander Roze Royss Jr,

I am writing to let you know that I am pregnant with your baby. You were the only one I have been with, and I am keeping it, so you better get used to seeing my pretty face. Also, you better tell this girlfriend of yours. If you don't, I will. I am sorry that it turned out this way. I will be filing for child support. I want you to think about us being a family. You do not need her, and I do not want her around our child. So again, tell the Bitch or I WILL!!!

Sincerely, Mrs. Future Zander Roze Royss Jr

I always knew that what I was doing would come back to haunt me. I treated women so badly and cheated on them like it was going out of style. And I messed around on my true love. I got her back, and I am about to lose her all over again. A baby?

How? I always used protection. I will have her take a paternity test; I don't believe her for a second. The problem is, if Noel finds out about this chick, it will ruin our relationship.

I called the housekeepers at the main mansion and told them to take care of this mess. I can't catch a break. My car is fixed, and I am about to head to work. I have a pressing case to handle. I need my life to get back to being great and stress free. Is the Roze Royss family cursed?

RING

"Hey, Love, I am on my way to the office. What's good?"

"Hey, Zanny, love. I just wanted to call you to tell you what happened to me today." Noel said.

"What happened."

"One of my colleagues said that my tires were flat. I went outside, and all four tires were flat. I have to start parking my car in the garage. It just saves so much time parking on the street. But oh well, I will have to keep my car off the streets because my enemies are always trying to get me. Lol lol"

"Wow, I am so sorry babe. Do you want me to get it fixed for you?"

"No, love. I already have someone down in the garage taking care of it. I just wanted to let you know. Today is going to be a long day. Well, I have to go. I have a call to take. Kisses."

"Kisses to you too."

The drama is already starting. Lavender!!

Chapter 21

ZADA ROZE ROYSS

So, my day is going pretty great. No, it's not. I am lying. I have to tell Raphael I am pregnant. This is going to be so hard, but I must tell him. At least he knows that I am not having sex with my soon-to-be ex-husband. My brother's girlfriend Noel is one of the best divorce attorneys out there, so I will talk with her about my situation soon. I feel like my world is going in slow motion with all that is going on right now. I am headed to Raphael's house to talk to him. I haven't seen him all week.

The gates opened to a beautiful estate with manicured lawns. I drove the round-a-bout and pulled up to the steps of the mansion. I take a deep breath before getting out of the car.

As I walked up the steps, I thought about being the lady of the house. It will be refreshing to be with a man who loves all of me versus one who can't stand the sight of me.

"Baby girl!" Raphael smiled from ear to ear. He met me at the door. "I've missed you." The hug was so genuine and touching.

"I missed you too, babe."

He knows about the things going on with my family, and he asked about it.

"Come on, let me get you comfortable. How is the family? Is everyone all right?"

"Yes, everyone is doing ok under the circumstances. It's hard to tell what everyone is thinking. We are all dealing with this in our own way. I am trying to be there for everyone, but I have my own issues to deal with. So, in saying that, we need to talk."

"Hold that thought. I have a surprise for you. Close your eyes."

"What?"

"Just close your eyes."

"Ok." I closed my eyes and was happy for the distraction.

He came up to me, grabbed my hand and pulled me to him.

"Don't open your eyes. In fact, wait right here. I need a scarf."

I heard his feet run away and then back again. He put the scarf over my eyes and guided me to this so-called surprise.

"Ok, watch your step, step 6 times. I'll help you."

"Where are you taking me?" I started to giggle.

"I said it's a surprise. Just relax and do as I say."

"Ok."

He started to graze his fingers up and down my arms. I started to get chills and giggle a little bit. He started to take off my clothes very slowly. I just embraced this feeling that I was all so familiar with.

"I am going to pick you up and lay you on your back, so don't panic when I lift you. I got you."

"Ok." I was getting excited because I love when he does these sorts of things. He is so thuggish but sweet and romantic at the same time.

"Are you ok?"

"Yes."

"Are you comfortable?"

'Yes, I am."

"Good. Do not move or take off your blindfold. I'm going to turn the air down. We'll need some cool air."

What is he trying to do to me? My heart is skipping beats, and I am warm all throughout my body.

"I'm above your head and about to take off your scarf."

He took the fold from my eyes.

What I saw was amazing. He had his room set up like a spa. There were roses on the spa bed I was lying on. Red, yellow, pink and white petals spread all over the floors. He had a rose gold garden tub with claw feet filled with bubbles waiting for me. He took a remote from his pocket and played my favorite song by Ms. Jonez Jody Macc called, you all should know by now, "The Elevator". He withdrew from his other pocket a peaches and cream body oil by Skinned, that smelled so intoxicating.

"Ok, now that you are in my castle, I want you to continue to lay back."

I surely did.

"Close your eyes."

Yes, yes, oh yes, I did.

I am glad I wore my hair just like he likes it, in an afro with a small headband. He removed my band as he stood over me to massage my head and temples. His fingers danced their way down the sides of my neck and outlined my collarbone. I quivered under his delicate touch like I always do, but for some reason, this felt different.

"I want you, Raphael," I whispered out of nowhere.

"Not yet." He stroked my nipples. He knows this is my hot spot. My breathing got heavier, and I couldn't catch my breath for a second. Am I about to cum? Wtf!

"Rub your pussy for me." It was like I was possessed or something. He continued to touch me and moved my hand for me to touch myself.

"I wanna see you cum for me."

I started to work on my moist center.

"Mmmmmm damn, this feels good."

"I know."

He took his finger and slowly traced it down my body until he got to the wet spot between my legs.

"Zada rub slow. We got all day."

I began to slow down.

"Damn, you look sexy as shit." He slipped his finger inside so easily and started to rub my inner core.

"O yes, baby."

"You like that, don't you?"

"Shit, yes."

He removed his finger and sucked on it like it was a cherry jolly rancher.

"I love the way you taste. It's mind-blowing. Keep playing with it."

"I'm about to cum."

"Yes, cum baby. I wanna eat it."

I put my hand on the back of his head, and he licked my pink wet pussy so good that my legs started to shake. I couldn't take it anymore.

"Raaaaa-pha-el! Aghhhh!" I released my sweet juices in his mouth.

"You taste so fuckin good." He picked me up from the table and laid me on the rose petal covered bed. He was out of his clothes in less than a second. He hovered over me with one motion and was deep inside me in seconds.

"Damn, you make me crazy." My scent intensified the vigor in his thrust as he moved inside my walls with controlled force.

I gripped his back with my nails, but that didn't stop him. He withdrew and flipped me on my stomach. His manhood slid back inside. He held my hands over my back and pounded my insides until I scream out his name.

"Raphael!"

He pulled me up on all fours and grabbed my waist with his massive hands and plowed into me like his life depended on it. It hurt, but it was a good kinda hurt. My husband never did shit like this.

"Fuck Yes!"

He was riding this horse with his experienced strokes.

"Goddammit!"

"Cum with me, baby. Let me know when you cumming." He spread my legs wider and opened me up even more so that he could dig deeper.

"Baby, it's cumin. Just keep doing that."

"Baby, keep going, keep going, oh shit, oh shit."

"Is that it, Zada? Tell me, baby is that it?" He thrust his penis in me like a drill, and that was it.

"That's it!!! Yes, baby, that's it."

"Hell, yeah, baby. Fuuuuuuuuuck!"

I squeezed him, and he went crazy.

"Oh, shit no, shit." I had him laying on top of me because my squeezing stopped him from moving.

"Ok, babe, let me go."

I loosened my grip, and he rolled over with me in his arms.

"Are you ok? I kind of went a little crazy for a minute. I just missed the hell out of you and that damn scent. I have to make a perfume out of that shit. I never loved a woman's smell so much."

Under my light brown skin, I know my cheeks were fire red from blushing.

"It turns me on to hear you rave about my smell like that."

"I bet. I have to make a song called, A Woman's Scent. That sounds nice."

"What would you put in it?" I was intrigued. He started to rap to me.

"Well, I would say something like......

Your essence drives me crazy

I'm ecstatic you my lady

Not playin

Just sayin

My woman's scent is amazin

Yo scent is greater than sex itself

You can have my money, all my wealth

There's only one woman, I'll never leave ha (Her)

Her name is Z A D A, that right Zada

I laughed, tickled pink because he was rapping about me. I loved this man so much, and to have his baby would be an honor. That's right! The baby.

"I love it, babe. Umm I need to talk to you about something."

"What's up, Red? I do not like those words."

"Well. It's nothing bad. I don't think."

"Ok, spit it out, Red."

And that's exactly what I did. I jumped out of bed like a damn track star. I ran to the bathroom and started puking like crazy.

"Zada! Babe! Are you ok? Babe! Open the door! Do you need me to call 911!"

I squeezed a no out barely. I guess he didn't hear me.

"I'm calling the ambulance."

"Raphael, no, I'm ok." I struggled to the door and opened it.

Before I hit the floor, he caught me.

"Damn, are you sure you're, ok? I can have my doctor check you out. He makes house calls."

"No, I'm fine. This is what I wanted to tell you."

"What are you ill? I know some of the best surgeons. What's up?"

I couldn't help but laugh. He is so cute when he is scared or nervous.

"Red, this shit ain't funny. What the fuck, man."

"Ok, can you help me get back to the bed and get me some orange juice? We can talk about it after that. Orange juice settles my stomach."

"Ok, bet."

After he did as I asked, he sat on the bed beside me and held my hands in his. I don't care how hard he is in the music world, in public or around his boys; he always shows me love and genuine care.

"Ok, babe, so first I want to say thank you for everything you did today. I really needed this stress reliever. I also came over to….."

"Wait, you are not breaking this off, are you?"

"Babe, relax. No, I am not."

"Ok, then spit the shit out, Red."

"I'm pregnant."

The room was silent. Raphael looked at me, but it looked like he was pissed more than happy.

"I have one question. Before I respond to what you just said, I need to know, have you slept with your husband and is it a possibility the baby is his?"

Now, I and all of you know that that is a valid question. Yawl know that I did not sleep with that crab of a man, you are my witness. However, I couldn't be mad with the question because I am still married.

"Babe, I swear, it's been well over a year that my soon-to-be ex-husband and I had relations. I promise you. When you and I decided to become serious, I took that to heart. My marriage ended a long time ago. So, no, it could not be his in any way, and yes, the baby is yours one hundred percent."

I saw his body relax and his lips slowly form into the biggest smile I have ever seen. He grabbed me and hugged me so tight.

"I knew it would be you and me forever." He let me go. "Does anyone else know?"

"Yes, my sister Zaniyah, but you don't have to worry about her. She won't say nothing."

"Well, I don't care if she says something. I'm waiting on you, but I don't want to mess things up for you either. So, in saying that, I am giving you thirty days to tell that muthafucka it is over, and you can stay here with me until things calm down. I am not missing out on being with you or seeing you carry my baby."

"Thirty days? That's not long enough, babe."

"How far along do you think you are?"

"About six weeks."

"Exactly, in a month, you will be ten weeks, that's the first trimester, right? I am not missing no more time after that."

"But Raphael….."

"No, I am not playing this time. If you don't tell him, I will. I will come to your house and shut that bitch down. So, decide."

Well, well, well. I guess I have some divorcing to do. Smh.

Chapter 22

ZANDRA ROZE ROYSS

I am just a stupid ole young girl who don't know nothing. How did I get myself in this mess? I didn't tell the father yet because I will be the one bringing on the drama this time when it comes out. The pregnancy is one thing, but the person who the baby is by is another. Now, it's been a while since I have spoken to you all about my drama because this family has enough going on. Everything has calmed down just a teeny tiny bit; I have to get you all updated.

So little dick Devin hasn't been in the picture for a while. I needed companionship, so I sought solace in someone else. I am pregnant with the someone else. Smh. My sister Zahara has been staying here with me a lot. She is living the life over here and she barely stays home.

I went to my father's study to talk to him about my situation so he could protect me from my mother, but what I heard made me stop in my tracks, listen and turn right back around. My dumb ass daddy had Beverly on speakerphone, so I heard everything.

"Zander, she is our daughter, not yours and Ziola's. She can't stay there like that. This is insane. It's bad enough that you put us in the middle of all your bullshit."

"Look, Beverly I am trying here. I can't help it if Zahara wants to be here. What am I supposed to do? Tell her no, you can't?"

"Ummm, yes, you dumb ass. I am always the bad person, so it's your turn. You tell her tonight is the last night."

"Fine, Beverly, fine."

"Oh yes, and when are you getting this so-called divorce? I've sat here for years waiting for you to decide. I have been cordial up to this point. You have until the end of this month to get your shit together, or I'll make your life a living hell, Zander!"

"Ok, I'll handle it. Just calm down."

"Calm down, my ass! I have dealt with this long enough! Get Your Shit Together and chose muthafucka!"

CLICK

Daaaaaaaaaaaaaamn. I never seen my dad so defeated. I can't tell him a damn thing. He can't even keep his side chick in check. I'll pass. I went back to my room.

Zahara came to my door, "Hey, are you ok? You look depressed."

"Yes, I am depressed. Come in and close the door. I don't want anyone to hear us."

I laid back on my bed looking at the ceiling, and my sister did the same.

"Zan, what are you thinking about?"

"A few things. One, I overheard your mom tell Dad that tonight is your last night staying."

"Wow, are you sure? Where did you hear that?"

"Just know that I know, and he will be talking to you soon, but I really don't want you to go."

"I'll handle it. I want to be here for you, and I get to drive us to school from here. My mom won't let me get near her Lexus."

We shared a sisterly laugh, and then it got serious again.

"I have to tell the father about this Zahara, and I am scared. Everyone is going to be so disappointed in me."

"Just think of it like this. This will be a learning lesson for you. First, stay away from sex, you are too young to be having sex, but since it's too late for that, you will have to look at this as an experience that you do not want to have ever again until you are old and mature enough to take care of matters on your own. I can't really give advice because I am too young myself, so, I don't know what I would do. But what I can do is be here with you all the way through. Even if everyone gets mad because I didn't say anything. So, in saying that, when are you going to tell your parents. You shouldn't keep this from them. You need medical attention."

"I know, and I don't know. Let me first tell my boyfriend that no one knows about. Oh boy."

"Do you want me to be here when you do it?"

"Yes, please."

"Ok. Just let me know when and I'll be here."

I got up to get my cell phone off my dresser.

"Wait! What? Now?"

"Yes, better now than never."

"Damn, why am I the one sweating? If he says the baby is not his, I swear we will drive over there and egg his house."

That made me laugh because I know she would do just that. She is my sister.

RING

"Hey, what's up, Zandy. What's good?"

"I need to talk to you about something important. Are you busy? I can call back?"

"Oh naw, I got time. When it comes to you, everything can wait."

I felt his smile through the phone. This is the co-captain of the basketball team. The one my brother specifically said to stay away from. The one that all the girls like, the one that flirts with all the girls, the one that likes to party, the one that my brother will disown, the one that my brother will want to kill, the one that's my brother's best friend.

"Alex, I'm pregnant."

I heard silence and then a dial tone.

Chapter 23

ZANDELL ROZE ROYSS

Everything that is going on with the family is making me feel all types of ways. I do not know whether to cry or to be happy. I like my new family, but I do not love them yet. I see smiles and chatter, but no one was upset except my baby sister, but now it seems like she is all up in Zahara's face. What is really going on? I feel like we shouldn't have to deal with this foolishness. I feel like no one cares about how I feel. My mom has been hanging out like a rock star, not cooking. Nope. She just doesn't give a ... Damn. There I said it. Damn damn damn damn damn.

My boy Alex has been over here like crazy. Which is cool because I need a friend to help me get through this. I think he likes my sister Zahara, but I already told him even though I do not like them at a hundred percent, he still needs to stay away from her. And he has.

RING

"Hey, what's up Al, are you coming tonight? I have a show picked out and everything."

"Yeah, um, about that. I can't come over tonight. My mom needs my help with something, but I'll come to the crib with you tomorrow after practice, and we can watch it after homework. Cool?"

"Ok, that's what's up. I wish you would have told me; I would have stayed with you. But it's cool. I'll see you tomorrow."

"Ok, cool. Out five thousand."

"Out five thousand."

Dang, well, that went down the tubes. Well, I guess I'll put on some porn and jack off. Being fifteen sucks. I need to make these millions to find the woman of my dreams and have sex all the time. But my hand will have to do for now.

Just as I started working on myself....

KNOCK KNOCK KNOCK

That knock scared the shit out of me.

"Shit."

"Did you say come in?"

"Um, hold up, Zandra." Goddammit, I put my member in my pants.

"Come in, Zandra."

She peeked her head in.

"Oh, Alex isn't here?"

"No, he is not, he will be here tomorrow, and you can play UNO then. Is that all you wanted?"

"Yes."

"Seriously? Man, go to bed."

"Awwww, I'm sorry for messing up your jack-off session. Good night." She shut the door before the pillow I threw could hit her in the damn face.

Damn now I have to start all over.

Chapter 24

Zander Roze Royss Sr

KNOCK KNOCK KNOCK

"Yes?"

"It's Dad. Are you decent?"

"Yes."

I walked in and looked at my lovely daughter Zahara, looking just like her older sisters. I was blessed to have a beautiful family. It didn't matter who birthed them.

"We need to talk."

"Ok. I'm all ears."

"Ok, do you like it here?"

"Yes, I do, Dad. Why?"

"Well, I wanted to let you know that your mother misses you and wants you back home. She is not too much of a fan of you being here with Ziola and me. It just doesn't sit well with her. And she wanted me and you to talk about it and to get you back home."

"Ok, well, dad, we talked about it, and my answer is that I want to stay here for right now. See, that was fast."

"No, Zahara, we have to talk about this properly. Why don't you want to go home?"

"I just don't."

"Ok, that is not an answer. Why don't you want to go home?"

"Because I need to be here for Zandra. She is going through something, and she needs me. I can't leave until her situation is resolved."

"Ok, Zahara, you and Zandra will be sisters forever. That is not going to change any time soon."

"No, that's not it. She is slowly coming to terms with us being sisters."

"Oh, so what is it then? You have to give me something. Does she need us? Did someone hurt her?"

"No one hurt her, and yes, she will need you soon. I would tell you, Dad, but it's a delicate situation. She needs to be the one to tell you."

"Ok, well, I am going to talk to her right now."

"Be careful. She heard a conversation from earlier between you and mom, so she might bite your head off when she sees you."

"Ok, so wish me luck. Your dad is about to make another woman mad."

She giggled. "Good luck."

I took the long walk to Zandra's room, my baby, my daughter that I am so close with. I didn't even see that something was wrong. If someone hurt her, I am going to kill them.

"Hey kiddo, it's dad. Are you decent?"

"Yes."

"Hey, what's good? We haven't talked in a while."

"I know."

Yup, she has an attitude. Her arms are crossed, and she got that neck rolling thing going on just like her mother right about now.

"Well, I would like to catch up with my baby girl. Like we use to before…."

"Before you decided to add another woman, three almost-grown kids and an on-the-way-baby in our lives?"

Damn, she sure put it out there.

"Wow. When you say it like that, it does sound horrible as it looks."

"Yes, it does."

"Listen, sweet-pea, I didn't mean to hurt you. I am so sorry. Tell me how you feel so I can address it. You can talk to me about anything, and I will do everything I can to not get upset. I promise."

"Ok, I was your baby girl, and now you are about to have another baby. I won't be your baby anymore. She or he will take my place."

"That will never happen. Yes, you will have another sibling, but that doesn't mean I will love you any less. Yes, I will be there for the baby, but you will too. You will be my big helper." For some reason, her face changed, she looked like she wanted to cry. I walked slowly to her bed and calmly sat by her side. I encircled her in my arms as she started sobbing.

"Zandra, what is wrong? Is it something else? I don't understand. Talk to me."

"I want mom!"

"She's not here."

"I want mom!" She continued to sob in between words. "Ok, let me reach her. "Zahara!!!"

Zahara ran in the room quickly,

"Yes, Dad! Oh, my goodness. What happened?"

"I don't know, and she won't tell me. She wants her mom. Come over here with her while I call Ziola. Rub her back to calm her down. You have to calm down, Zandra, before you have a panic attack like your brother. Try to relax." Zandra started wailing.

I heard Zahara whispered to her sister while I called Ziola.

"Listen, Zandy, you have to just spit it out and say it. This is not healthy for you. You're going to have a nervous breakdown."

"I…. want….. my ….mom…!"

Ziola finally answered her phone with her new fucked up attitude.

"What the fuck do you want, Zander? What the hell is that in the background?"

"You need to get here quick. Something is wrong with Zandra, and she's crying and going crazy. She is calling for you. She's not talking to nobody."

"Ok, I am on my way."

Zandra's eyes were swollen with her face beet red. She kept sniffling and couldn't stop crying.

"Your mother is on her way." I heard Zahara say.

Zandell rushed into the room sweating. "Dad, what is going on?"

"I don't know. Something is wrong with your sister, and she won't talk unless your mother is here."

"I called the family over; I didn't know what else to do."

"Thanks, son."

In about 30 minutes, everyone started walking through the door at the same time. Zaniyah, Zada, Zander Jr and the lady of the house, Mrs. Ziola Roze Royss. Everyone ran up the stairs.

"Ok, I'm here," Ziola stated.

"I only want my mom." Zandra sniffled.

"Ok, love, everyone, get out of the room, please."

The family was in the loft, waiting for a response to what the hell was going on. If it's not one thing, it's another.

Everybody is talking and asking Zahara questions, and she is not saying a word. Then we heard a screech.

"What!"

Five minutes later, Ziola walked out of the room, and we all stood up. She walked past us to her room, grabbed her pillow and a blanket. She bypassed us again to go back into Zandra's room. She turned around and looked at everyone before she went inside.

"You can all go back home to your respected beds. Please be here tomorrow for dinner at 7 pm. Please do not disturb Zandra and me tonight. Do not call or text. Just be here tomorrow on time. Zandra is pregnant. Good night." She turned and walked into Zandra's room and locked the door.

Our faces hit the floor. Nobody said anything. We just stared at each other, and tears dropped from Zaniyah and Zada's eyes. Jr looked pissed, and Zandell look was priceless.

I looked at Zahara and I couldn't hold back any longer.

"Zahara! Who is the father? I know you know. So, spill it now!"

"I can't…"

"No! The story is out now, so who is the father!'

"Uuuuuuuuum… it's Zandell's best friend, Alex."

That's when I lost it. My son and I said the same thing at the same time. "Oh, hell naw!!!"

Chapter 25

Zandell Roze Royss

Well, well, well. Today is going to be a great day at school for me. I feel like I am on top of the world. My life feels like shit, and I feel like tearing some heads off. How about that world? I wanna tear some shit up. How dare he come to my house and screw my sister. Oh no, not the sixteen, twenty, or even the twenty-five-year sister. Oh no! These punk muthafucka skips three sisters and aim for the fuckin baby! I am piiiiiiiissed! It's on today.

"Hey! What's up, Bro!" Alex said as he walked up to me to give me dap.

BOOM!!! I knocked the shit out of Alex. He hit the floor, I jumped on top and started wailing on him. All the oohs and the aghhs were coming from all the kids in the hall. The crowd started getting thicker, but the only thing on my mind was, I'mma kill you, and that's exactly what I would have done if the school security and two teachers didn't get me off him.

Alex was bleeding, and it looked like he had a black eye and busted nose already. In a rage, I started yelling, trying to get loose to get to Alex and finish him off.

"Get off me!"

"Yeah, let that punk bitch go!" Alex was up on his feet now. They had to take us to the principal office separately because I was still trying to get at him.

Once in the office, Principal Jones just stared at me for a few moments to give me a minute to calm down. He saw the rage in my eyes and the anger dripping from my face.

"Zandell, you are one of my best students at this school, and I have never had a problem out of you. So, whatever this is, it must be something bad. I know you are angry, and you may have every right to be. However, this is my school, and it's my job to keep everyone, regardless of whatever they have done, safe. You have violated that today in the worst way. I have to call your parents, his parents, and hopefully, they don't press charges. He is getting checked out now, so let's hope you didn't do too much damage, young man."

"Honestly, I don't care if I did."

"Ok, no remorse, huh? Alright. Let me call your parents before you say something, you may regret."

When I saw my father walk through the doors of the principal office, I knew he wasn't mad at all. Actually, I think I saw him smirk a little, but he straightened himself up right before talking to the principal. Of course, he had to put on his poker face.

"Hello Principal Jones, I am so sorry I had to come here under these circumstances."

"I know Mr. Roze Royss. Please have a seat."

My father looked at me and then back at the principal.

"So, we have a problem here. The altercation your son was in this morning has brought on much concern. I am thinking of expelling Zandell due to the damage he has done to Alexander Mitchell. Mr. Mitchell looks to possibly have a fractured nose and a black eye. Zandell outright attacked him in front to multiple witnesses. This is a huge problem for me, Mr. Roze Royss. I will have to suspend him for ten days, but I have to consider expulsion as well."

"I understand, Principal Jones, but can we please reconsider the expulsion? I understand the suspension, but the expulsion is a bit much. I do not agree with his behavior, but can we come to an agreement of some sort, and I will make sure that this doesn't happen again? Our family is going through a bit of a rough time right now, and Mr. Mitchell is involved."

"I don't know about that, Mr. Royss."

"It's Mr. Roze Royss." My father's tone was unnerving and threatening.

My father spoke kindly to me.

"Ok, son can you excuse Mr. Jones and I for a moment? Just wait outside the door."

"Sure, Dad." I got up and stepped out, but I had the door slightly cracked.

"Mr. Royss, I mean Mr. Roze Royss let me explain…"

"No. You don't get to explain nothing. It's my turn to talk. Now I have tried to be polite, but it seems like you are having fun throwing around this expulsion idea, so let me break this down to you. The suspension is fine; however, expulsion is off the table, period point-blank. No one gave a damn about this school until my son gave the people something to talk about, from his 5.5 GPA to his professional future NBA skills. Not to mention all the money I put into this school. Yes! That part! This is my son's first mishap, so I am telling you to make something happen, or your school will go back to being the nothing that it was."

"Ok, ok, ok, fine. I will see what I can do, but this can never happen again, or you will have to take that money…"

"I got it. Leave it alone, Jones. I said it will never happen again." My father got up to leave. My dad did his thing. I am glad because I felt a little bit bad about hurting my friend to that level. But it had to be done. He betrayed me and played on my kindness.

"Come on, son."

"Yes, Sir."

In the car, everything was quiet at first. You could hear a pin drop. I could tell that my dad was not one hundred percent upset but was still bothered.

"Son, I understand your frustration. First off, someone violated your sister, no someone messed with your sister. It wasn't right, but it's true. I still can't get over that, but anyway, someone messed with your sister and most importantly, it was your best friend. So, I get why you're mad. But you could have come to me before doing what you did at school. You could have done some serious damage to your friend and put yourself in jail. You could have killed him, messed up your life, your career. Never do that again unless we talk first. Ok?

"Ok, Dad. I was just mad, and I couldn't see reason. I just saw red."

"I know, but we could have handled that better. Now, I know you're not going to like this, but you will apologize. I know. It is killing me to say that, but I am trying to avoid a lawsuit here. We will pay the medical bills, but a lawsuit is the last thing we need right now. Ok? And he is your best friend. You may be mad now, but he is still your friend. You two may not talk for a while, but you've known him since the age of five. It's sickening to say, but at least your sister chose someone that we know and trust. God, that sounds horrible."

"It does." We both laughed, and I was grateful for it because it was getting too serious, and I did feel kind of bad about hurting Alex.

"So, when we get home and get settled, I'll call Alex's parents. I wouldn't be surprised if they aren't at our house already...."

My father spoke it right up. Alex's mom was standing outside their car right in front of the house. Damn. I should have known because Alex's mother doesn't play. Shit. All my family was standing outside too.

"Stay in the car Zandell."

My dad jumped out and immediately tried to defuse the situation.

"Angie, I was going to call you. I don't think it's a good idea that you are here."

"I tried to tell her Mr. Zander, but she wouldn't listen," Alex replied.

"Shut the fuck up, Alex! Zander, you're telling me to let this shit go. Have you lost yo damn mind? Zandell, get yo ass out of the car! Now!"

"Ok, Angie, let's talk about this calmly."

"Talk calmly, my ass! Zandell, get out of that damn car!"

My mother stepped in.

"Let's talk about this inside Angie."

Angie yelled.

"Hell no! Did you want to talk about this shit this morning before Zandell put his foot in my son's ass? Huh?"

The look on Alex's face was of total embarrassment.

"Well, Ma, he didn't put his foot in my ass."

Angie looked at her son with both love and anger.

"Yes, he did and didn't I tell you to shut the fuck up! I got this. And Ziola, if Alex would have done this to Zandell, you would be doing the same damn thang, so I don't want to hear it!"

My brother and sisters stood by watching this circus. It just looked like everyone was just tired at this point. I got out of the car and started to walk over to Mrs. Angie. If she was going to hit me, then so be it because I know what I did was wrong. I detoured and walked slowly up to Alex to show that I come in peace. I stood ten feet away from him just to show that I do not want to fight.

"Listen, Man, Alex, I am sorry for jumping on you like that this morning. You messed with my sister, not one of my older ones, but my baby sister? How could you do me like that? Like, seriously?"

He looked down for a second with shame written all over his face.

"I'm sorry too. I don't know what got into me. Your sister is a little pushy, so I rode with it, which is no excuse. I shouldn't have crossed that line, and I am sorry about that. You are my best friend, and I should have told you, versus giving in to the temptation. My bad, bro."

"I accept your apology. So, my next question is what's up with you and my sister? Are you trying to take care of the baby, or are you walking away?"

"Now you know I would never do that. I'mma take care of mines."

"Ok. This is stupid. I haven't fully forgiven you yet, but you are still my boy. Shake on it?"

"Yeah." We hugged it out.

"Ouch, man. Watch my face."

"Oh, my bad. Damn, I fucked you up."

He punched me in my arm. "Shut up, man, you know if I would have saw that coming, I wouldn't be looking like this. Now, I got to fight a few cats at school to show that I ain't no punk."

"Again, my bad. So now that we are good, let's try to stop our parents from trying to kill each other." Right as I said that everyone got quiet, so we looked in the direction of Ms. Angie, and the look on her face reminded us that she didn't know about the baby.

"Alex, you did what and to who?"

"Ma, I am so sorry. I didn't..."

"What in the hell?"

I didn't know my sister didn't go to school today, so when she screamed from the porch over everybody, she scared the hell out of us.

"Everybody, just stop it! Just stop! This is too much!"

My sister Zada yelled in a panic, "Zandra! Your bleeding!"

Zandra looked down, right along with everyone else. She saw the blood cascading down her legs. The look of horror and fear in her face, as she looked back up at us, must have overwhelmed her because she fainted and hit the ground.

Chapter 26

ZANDRA ROZE ROYSS

Monitors were buzzing, ventilators going. I faintly heard Zada, Zaniyah and my mother frantic talking in rushed tones. Doctors were all around me. It sounded like my father and brothers were yelling at the medical staff. I was going in and out. Why was everyone in a panic? What's happening to me? I heard a machine start beeping loud and fast. The doctors were telling my family to get out and leave, but why? Suddenly, an excruciating pain shot through my stomach.

"Agggghhhhhhhhhh!"

The nurse is starting to push everyone out of the room. "Please, everyone get out!"

"Mommy!! Aghhhhhhh!" What the fuck is this pain? My brain couldn't understand what my body was going through. My stomach felt like it was ripping into two.

"Let me go!" My mom finally fought through and held my hand.

"It will be ok, baby, just relax."

I saw tears rolling down her eyes. I never saw her cry before. Am I dreaming? I started to drift in and out again because the pain was so unbearable.

"I love you, baby girl."

As darkness kissed my soul like a soft touch a of a baby's bottom, those were the last words I heard.

Walking down the spacious corridor, I see such a beautiful white light, grow bigger and bolder with every step. I heard something but couldn't see it because of the blinding light, so I continued down the path. Suddenly the corridor turned into a field full of beautiful green grass with yellow, pink, purple, and peach flowers blooming as I walk forward. I see children to my left playing double dutch, and two people sitting at a table playing chess. The elderly man had a salt and pepper beard, and the other person was a little brown girl that looked around the age of five. I looked at the man weird and I instantly went into protective mode. Instead of playing with the kids, she is siting with this grown man.

"Hello sir, is this pretty little girl your daughter?"

He looked at me with a scold on his face like I disgusted him. "No, she is not."

Ok now I must call for help. This is kidnapping, I can feel it.

"Hello little girl. What's your name?"

"I don't have a name."

"Well of course you do, how old are you?"

"I don't have an age."

Ok enough is enough.

"Where are your parents?" She looked at me and tears started to fall down her chunky brown cheeks.

"What's wrong? Did you kidnap her?" I accused the man.

In his deep baritone voice, he spoke.

"No, I did not."

"What is going on here? I am going to call the police."

"There are no police here."

"Come on let's go find your parents." I touched her hand, my whole body got warm as flash backs started to come to my mind with being pregnant, I looked down at my stomach and it was flat. What the...... Looking down at the little girl with sadness beaming from her pretty light brown eyes, with a teddy bear in her arms, my soul ached. I felt a connection with her for some reason. I realized at that moment that the teddy bear the little girl was holding was the same teddy I had growing up. Is this me when I was younger? No, It, can't be. I remember when I got pregnant that I said I would pass it down to my ...... daughter????

The old man interrupted my thoughts. "Now do you want to know why she has no name or no age?

My eyes gave him my answer.

"Because she died before she was even able to move in her mother's womb."

"What? I don't understand."

"Your right you don't understand. Your too young to understand. Do you remember ever losing a baby? Miscarriage?"

"Miscarriage? What is that?"

"When a woman, or in your case, little girl gets pregnant and there is a sudden loss of pregnancy. You're way too young to have a baby. Thirteen? Your body can't take it. Just young and dumb."

Then it hit me like a ton of bricks. Bright lights, cheerful children, beautiful garden and flowers blooming as I walk! My daughter!

"Wait! Where am I? What is this place?"

"Look around my Dear." He bellowed in laughter. "What does it feel like?"

"I would say heaven but I know I didn't die........" I started to look around again at the plush green grass with perfect yellow, red, pink, white and purple flowers. The rich trees with strong limbs, the children that continued to laugh and jump rope with no care in the world. Right at this very moment gold platinum gates started to appear and open. Everything stopped. The girls stopped jumping and started towards the gates. The old man got up and started to make his way to the gate as well. My so-called daughter got up from her table to run and catch up with the old man to hold his hand. She tugged on his shirt first to stop him, and he stopped. She looked back at me and smiled warmly, waved goodbye, turned and skipped with the old man right through the gold gates.

I don't want to go. I'm too young to die. Why am I here? I grabbed my chest as all my memories came flooding back. I lost my baby, but I was just a baby myself. I heard my name, as I looked up at the old man and my daughter, they were waving at me to join them. The man started to suddenly look familiar. He was my great great grandfather. I remember the pictures in my father's study. Oh no. I am in heaven.

"I want to go but I can't right now." I shouted.

"I don't know what this is, but I don't want it! Not now. I want my life back! I promise to be good God or whoever is running this ship!" Omg I am saying all the wrong things.

"No, I wanna go home! Mommy! Mommy! I wanna go home! Ma!"

Ziola jumped out of her chair and ran to her daughter's side as tears streamed down her face. "Mommy is here baby. I'm right here." She held Zandra tight.

"Ma it's you! Ma I am so sorry! I'm so sorry! I died Ma. I saw great great grandpa and my daughter. What happened?"

"Um well, baby you had a miscarriage. I am so sorry."

"Nooooooooooooo nooooooooooo! Where is she? Nooooooooo!" The doctors had to come in and sedate me. I know I was too young, but I saw what she could have grown up to be! Her eyes were like mines, I wanted to redeem myself and now I can't. I wanted to start fresh and raise her to be better than me, I needed to tell her I love her, I wanted to show her I will be there for her no matter what. My baby is gone, she is really gone! My dream was real. Why did God take her from me! Why! The only thing I could do was yell. "Why did you take her from me! Why!"

Chapter 27

ZANDELL ROZE ROYSS

I felt so bad for my sister. Man, she looked bad. She will be needing some professional help. Thirteen, pregnant and then a losing a baby? Wow, I am sure that is a lot on a person's mental health. While the hospital kept her for a few days, we all decided to have a funeral for the baby. After her discharge, we helped her get on her feet and prayed that she would be mentally ready for the burial we put together.

The way that my mom set up the funeral was to die for. Oops! I meant to say that the funeral was well put together. My mother had an assortment of white lilies that she said represented innocence of the soul. They were everywhere and in all colors. Wreath, crosses, hearts and plants were along the garden, there wasn't a casket, of course, but Zandra had an engravement done on a soft satin pillow that said,

"To my Dear Zanelle Mitchell, you will never be forgotten and will always be loved by your mother and father.

Zandra Ross Royss and Alexander Mitchell."

Man, you would have thought that the baby lived a full life with how my sister was carrying on. Maybe I don't understand. You will have to forgive me, but dang. A lot of people came too, which is crazy, I believe they were just nosey, but I am happy they are here to support my sister. Zandra and Alex were sitting in the front. Just watching them sitting together, knowing what he did to my sister is starting to make my blood boil. I am going to find a hiding place and lay low.

I started to make my way to my room, but so many people kept stopping me. So, I went into my mother's room. Today is taking a toll on me because I am trying to be empathic to my sister's needs and situation, but I believe I'd be dead if it was me. And I meant to use the word dead, this time. My sister is literally getting away with murder.

Zandra was telling me how she saw the gates of heaven and how exquisite it looked. My sister was kind of out of it in the hospital, especially after she found out she lost the baby. She almost took the doctors and nurses heads off. I knew she was strong, but not that strong. Geesh.

♣

Lying on my mother's bed with my head upon her soft pillows, I wondered about my life. I can't wait to get out of here, go to college and then the NBA. I am tired of my family's drama. I don't mean to sound insensitive, but every time I turn around, there's some other shit going on. I may need psychological help myself.

Even Jr is looking like he's clean and clear, but little do he know, I saw that girl who came out of his house and spray-painted WHORE on his car. I didn't call the police or him for that matter because it was funny as hell. I knew she wouldn't hurt him for real, and I knew who it was. I've seen all of Jr's girls.

Mom's pillow feels a bit lumpy which is weird. As I started to adjust the pillow to make me more comfortable, a journal hit the floor. The book fell open, so I reached down to pick it up to put it back under the pillow, but a few words jumped out at me.

I will take this to my grave.

Wooo. What is mom talking about? I locked the door, went to the balcony, and peeked out to look for mom. She was sitting with Alex's mother, so I was good. I ran to the bed, grabbed the book, and started to read. What I read blew my mind. I am speechless.

He keeps beating me, and I don't know why. I never did anything to him but love him. I can't cook good enough, walk good enough, talk good enough nor sex him good enough. I am trying so hard to be the woman he wants me to be. I haven't told anyone, but I am pregnant again. I can't believe that this has happened. I know it's not his, and I can't tell the real father because if the real father found out, he would want to be a part of his baby's life. I have to keep this secret. I will take this to my grave! Plus, my husband would hurt me worse than he's ever done before.

I have to protect my baby and I won't let him beat it out of me. I would have never stepped out if he would have just treated me like he did when we first met. I don't know what happened to him; he gets off on punching or even pinching me in places no one can see. I also have to wear makeup all the time because you will see the scars and bruises, he leaves on me. And forcing me to have sex with him. The raping is torture...

BOOM!

I slapped the book shut. Muthafucka!!! Lies, lies, and more lies, secrets, secrets, and more fuckin secrets. See! I need a doctor too! When I get mad, I see red, and there is another side of me. One of us is created out of wedlock, and you beat my mom!!! Not only that, but you also sexually assaulted her! Ok!

My rage boiled like a volcano ready to erupt. I left my mom's room in a frenzy. As I walked through the crowd, people spoke to me, but I didn't hear a word. The only thing I heard was my mind saying, fuck that muthafucka up! Zander Sr, you are a lying piece of shit! This family sat around for years dealing with yo tempers, attitudes, and yo want-us-to-be-perfect-because-that's-how-the-Roze-Royss-family-get-down cocka-doodle bullshit lines your always spittin at us. I knew something was wrong with my mother, I just knew it.

Thinking about all the smiles she put on her face every day in front of us, how we laughed with her and all the while this beast-of-a-fucka hurt her? Well, never again. I don't care what my mother did. This bastard had a whole family outside of my mom in which she still is woman enough to smile about it.

Zandell could only see red as he looked upon the crowd searching for his dad.

Perfect, mostly everybody was in the house and the whole immediate family is outside surrounding punk ass Alex and my tired ass looking sister. I punched the palm of my hand, I needed it to wake up because I am about to fuck a bitch up! I shoulder bumped my way through everybody because I only saw him. I wanted to get to him.

"So! You like to hit women huh?" My father looked perplexed and stared directly at my mom like, "Did you really tell him that?"

"Nah, you don't have to look at her. Look at me! So, you like to hit women, huh?"

"Son, what are you talking about? No, I don't." I saw the weak ass look on his face like oh shit, my son done found out.

Zander Jr chimed in with, "Dell, are you ok? Do you need a drink? Let's take a walk and talk about what's gotten you so riled up....."

Right before Jr was able to get through the crowd to me, I punched Sr right in the face and started wailing on him. Sr didn't stand a chance; he didn't see it coming.

All the brothers, Jr and the twins tried to get me off him. He had a bloody nose lying on the ground, and only Beverly tried to help my dad get up.

Holding an unexpected bloody nose, Zander Sr yelled, "What the fuck!"

"If you put your hands on my mother again, I'mma kill you nigga! I'mma kill you!"

Jr and the twins were standing in front of me, trying to hold me back. It's hard to restrain me when I get this upset. I know my brother was glad the twins were there because Jr was having a hard time constraining me. Zain finally helped Beverly hold Sr back and started to walk him off to a secluded area because people started to see what all the commotion was about. Just like I said, I have to get the fuck away from this family. I can't take it no more.

Chapter 28

Zaniyah Roze Royss

What the fuck just happened? What the fuck is going on? Did I just see my fifteen-year-old brother punch the fuck out of dad! Yes, I did. I love dad, but that was so deserving. He should have gotten that with all the shit he keeps putting us through. Especially if what Dell is saying is true. I looked at my mother, and tears started to fall from her eyes. Zandra, Zada and I walked up to her at the same time, hugged her, and that's when she boo hoo cried.

"Mom, people are coming out. Let's go to your room and get away from all of this?"

In between sniffles she mustered, "Zaniyah and Zada, can you please tell everyone to leave."

"Ok, Ma. We're on it."

As my mother walked back in the house, walked through all the whispers and people trying to see what's wrong, I heard my sister's big mouth telling everyone they don't have to go home, but they got to get the hell out of the Roze Royss mansion.

We got to my mother's room, and she saw an open book on her bed.

"Oh my God!! Zandell read my journal!"

"Mom, it's just a journal."

"No, you don't understand!"

Whatever my brother read from her journal must not have been good because as Zaniyah walked into the room with Zandra, my mother started to cry again.

"Zandra, maybe you should wait outside."

Zandra didn't move. "I want to know what's wrong with mom. I can handle it. What's wrong? Did daddy do those things that Dell said he did?"

I knew this would be hard for Zandra because she is daddy's favorite, and he is hers. I felt so horrible about this for her, but we are a family, and we have to get through it as a family.

"Ok, you can stay but just chill until we get to the bottom of this."

"Ok." She sat in one of my mother's chairs with a scared look on her face and was quiet. Ok, she is good, so now let me help Zada with our mother. My mom couldn't stop crying. It seemed like she was crying for all the years of the heartache she has been through.

My mother was lying on her left side with her pillow in a death grip.

"Ma, listen, I can't say that I know what you are going through and how you are feeling. But there is one thing for sure. It doesn't matter how bad it is, we love you so much, and we would never laugh at your pain or hate you for the things that happened. You have your own reasons for everything you do or did. We are only here to hear you and be here for you. Do you understand, ma? We are not here to judge you."

Zada finally caught on to what I was doing and started to help.

"Yes Ma, Zaniyah is right. No judgment. You are our mother at the end of the day, and all we want to do is to be here for you. Ma, are you ok?"

Ziola turned to the girls and padded her side for Zandra to join them on the bed.

In a shaky voice full of pain. "I did something despicable, and I don't know what to do. I have done some things that you all may never forgive me for."

"Mom. Zada, Zandra and I will love you regardless. Just talk to us so we can help you get through it. Dad is gone. He went for a ride. You have time so just relax. Do you want us to give you some space or…"

"No, please stay."

"Ok, we will stay."

"I need to tell you girls something, and again, you may not like it."

"Ma, we are here with you through it all." The look of dread on my mother's face showed how ashamed she was of whatever she felt she needed to tell us. And so, the story began.

We were all in and waiting to hear the new drama that this family will endure. I felt sorry for my mom because if my father did what he did to her, then she has been living a nightmare for as long as she can remember. Also, the worse part of it is, she had all of us to help to protect her and we never did.

She has three girls and two strong boys who could fought for her. Me, alone, could have taken my father out with my iron bat that I always leave in my trunk, the taser that's on my key chain or the twenty-two that's in my glove compartment. Yes, I am licensed to carry. I am a female on a college campus, so damn straight I am packing in various ways. Finally, I can fight my ass off. I'm a Roze Royss, I can handle myself. Wow, that name is not sounding so strong anymore.

"Well, girls, do you have any questions?"

Zaniyah started because the thought was burning into her brain.

"Did dad hit you? Is this abuse true?"

My mother got off the bed and stood in front of us. She took off her dress. The scars that we saw were unspeakable. They were all in places we would have never seen on any given day. There were pinch marks on her arms, bite marks around her chest area and light welts on her back and butt. They were permanent scars of years of assault. We were speechless. She put her dress back on and walked into the bathroom. She came back out with her makeup remover and started to remove her makeup in spots that had permanent scares, but they were light as well. Her eye was a little dark due to the lashing she got right before this Beverly situation. However, it looks like it is going away. She also had a red mark that was finally fading away on her cheek. That's why the makeup was so important.

"Your father did not like to hit me in my face much, but whenever I got too mouthy with him, he would. My face has always healed, so no worries, girls, these other wounds will be healed soon." The sadness on her face was beyond what I can explain. I was fuming on the inside. I wanted to give my dad a TKO just like Zandell did.

Zandra had tears just falling from her eyes but didn't say a word. She knew this was hard for mom as did all of us.

Zada chimed in. "Mom, I am not judging in any way; I just want to know how this got this bad?"

"At first, it was little things like pushing me or just grabbing my skin and no pinching. It gradually got this bad. When you love someone, and they tell you that their sorry, you believe them over time, a person can break you down if you let them. I was so strong when your father and I met. But I was strong with the wrong one. It was weird at first but overnight, your father changed, and now I know why, it wasn't him. It was his twin. He hurt me out of anger by living a life he did not want."

Zada stated,

"But either way it goes, that doesn't make what he did to you right. He signed up for that, so he decided to do what comes with it, and he shouldn't have taken that out on you. Plus, you had his children."

"I know. I am not making excuses for him anymore. You are right. That's why I took full advantage of him having another family and filed for a divorce."

Zandra gasped, and we all turned to her. We weren't paying any attention, but she was reading mom's book.

"Mom, did dad rape you? How? You're married?"

"Zandra! Give me that." Mom snatched the book back. Zandra was able to read enough to look confused.

Zada asked,

"Mom, we are tired of secrets. What's in there?"

The look on Zandra's face told Ziola that she could not take her secret to her grave.

"Ma, which one of us is not daddy's child?"

Zada jumped from the bed and looked like she'd been shocked by a ten thousand bolt taser.

"Mom, what the hell is she talking about?"

I started to think to myself that I didn't know what was going on but by the question, I can see that Zander Sr did not birth someone. However, it doesn't matter about the question that was asked, I don't want to get too crazy in front of mom. I want her to remain calm to get the information that we need to move forward, so I am trying not to get mom riled up. I guess my sister forgot, so I had to remind her.

I gave her a look that said to calm and sit her having-a-husband-and-pregnant-by-another-man-ass down before I split her raggedy ass in two. She caught my drift and kindly sat down and changed her tone.

"Sorry mom. Can you tell us what's going on? Please."

Zandra chimed in finally.

"Mom please tell us." Ziola was defeated at this point.

Zada breathed in deeply and breath out to steady her heart. She took her mother's hands in hers and said what she'd been wanting to tell her family for a while now.

"Mom, I am somewhat in the same situation as you. My husband and I have been in separate beds for over a year. I am in the process of finding a great attorney to help me with my divorce because I am ready to move on. Also, I have fell in love with a man by the name of Raphael Lovechild, and to top it off, I just found out I am having his baby."

Zada held her breath waiting for what her mother might say to her. Disappointment, great sadness, angry, mad, etc. But what she got was totally not what she expected.

"Zada, I am so happy for you. I was so sick of your husband anyway; he is a leech who was sucking the life out of you. I will help you with this divorce, but it will be tough because you committed adultery but don't worry, Jr's lady Noel is handling my case. I'll get her on yours too."

"Wow, I wasn't expecting that. Thanks, Mom."

Zandra kindly spoke up. "Zada, are you talking about AKA Ca$h?"

"Yes, I am."

"Ok, we will talk about this later, but mom, can you please tell us who is not daddy's child? Is it me?"

Ziola spoke calmly,

"Sweetheart, Sr is your dad."

"Then who?"

I guessed first.

"Is it me? Just say which one of us it is, mom."

Ziola began to speak on the matter,

"I once fell for this NBA player by the name of Creon Travis Thompson."

I know who that is. "Mom, he plays for the Clippers, right?"

"Yes, that is correct."

I continued,

"The one that use to always get into fights with the other players and curse out the referees? Him?"

"Yes, that's correct."

I was amazed.

"Ok, ok, ok. So, let me get this right and see if I understand this. All of us are great athletes, and don't get me wrong, we have the athletic gene, but Zandra and Zandell have the pro athletic gene and if Zandra is dads, then that leaves Zandell? Our future NBA superstar? Mom? Is it Zandell?"

Ziola went quiet to gather her bearings and nervously spoke. "Yes, it is."

"Holy shit! Does Creon know about Zandell? Sorry mom I couldn't express it any other way."

"It's ok and I understand it's a shock. Yes, he does. Creon has been in his son's life the whole time, Zandell just doesn't know it, and neither does your father."

"Well, jol-fuckin-ly." I couldn't help it. I had to say it.

Chapter 29

Zandell Roze Royss

I got that airy feeling again like someone was watching me. I shook it off and thought about the situation at hand. I was whisked away by my brother and Noel. I was sitting in the back seat just fuming. My temper was slowly coming down, but damn, I was so mad. Why am I the only one in this damn family that has hidden anger issues? It's weird, I don't know where it comes from, but I just take it one temper at a time. Therefore, I like to be calm and not get into a mess. I like to stay to myself and don't like trouble, but trouble finds me. I just hate the fact that my dad is a monster, and I didn't know it. But what I am fuming about is that we did not see it.

"Did you know Jr?"

"Now, Dell, do not try to turn your anger on me. Hell, no, I didn't know! Do you think I would have allowed that to happen? Hell, fuck no! I apologize, Noel, when we get to the house, we will take this convo in the game room, but for now, it is what it is. Sorry."

"It's ok, I understand," Noel said.

I continued.

"Jr, how did we not see this? I knew something was going on. No man talks to his woman that way and not, at least once, put his hands on her. Mom was always jumpy. She was always careful with her words; she would look at Sr before and after she would speak as if she was silently getting his approval. That son of a bitch. I wanna kill him."

"How do you know about signs of abuse, Dell?"

"I pulled it up on my phone after I looked at mom's journal. I wanted to see if she showed any signs."

"Her journal?"

"Yes. She has a journal with all these secrets, along with things that has happened to her that she claims she will take to her grave, but I read them. One of the things was that one of us is not birthed by Sr."

Jr pushed on breaks. I am glad we were at his house already.

"What? Who?"

"Mom wrote down in her journal how she was pregnant again, and she knew that the baby wasn't dad's."

"We need to find out who."

"Why is that important? I mean at this point; I hope it's me because I don't want any of Sr's horrible traits. Well, Noel, you are good. Jr wouldn't hurt a fly."

She started to laugh like I didn't know what I was talking about. I am glad she is ok with all of this. I would want to run if I was her.

"Anyway, let's go inside and hit the game room. Let's get your mind at ease so you can calm down and see how we are going to confront mom about all this."

Once inside the house, Noel went her way, and we went upstairs to the game room to finish talking.

"So, Jr, what do you make of this dad and Mom situation? I am furious. We will not be able to stay in the same house. Not at all."

"I really don't know. I am a lawyer, but we are dealing with our family here. We have to be very careful in how we treat this. One good thing about this is that dad committed infidelity before mom did. Even if he says he didn't, he has kids to prove it, so whichever one of us who is not dad's, it really doesn't matter. Mom will still get child support and alimony. She will walk away with a lot of cash. So big ups for dad in that aspect for financially taking care of the family. Mom may get paid for pain and suffering because of her mental and physical abuse. I hope Beverly loves dad because from what it looks like, dad is about to be broke from my end, but I truly believe dad will be good. Mom can put that waiting-to-exhale-Angela-Bassett-money-move on'em."

Both laughed. Zandell remembered when his mom made Zandra and him sit to watch that movie with her. Because of my sisters and mother, I really tried to understand women more. I am a guy, I will never know about a woman fully, but I will do my best to empathize with them. Especially if it's one of my sister's or my mother.

I need to reach out to mom.

"I need to call mom to see if she is ok."

DING DONG!

"Zanny! Dell! Your mother and sisters are here!"

"Dang Dell, that's crazy."

"Tell them to come up here, please!" Jr shouted.

The footsteps of the women, as they ascended the stairs, gave me a feeling of wanting to protect. I stood to my full six feet and folded my hands in front of myself like a man who is ready for war.

"Hello, guys!" The girls said.

We hugged our mother immediately and then hugged our sisters. As the sisters walked Jr to the side to talk, my mother took my hand and walked me over to the bar so we could have a bit of a private moment. I know she probably wanted to tear me a new one because I punched my dad, but I would not change what I did for nothing. He got what he deserved.

I was so concerned. "Ma, are you ok? I couldn't stay because I needed to calm down, and Jr made me come here."

She took her hand and caressed the side of my face like she always did when my temper got the best of me, just like a mother should. "Yes, I am fine. But I need to talk to you. We can go into the guest room if you don't want to talk in front of everyone." She whispered.

"No, we have all kept enough secrets. I am fine with my brothers and sisters being here. They can help me through anything."

"Ok, if you want."

"But before we talk in front of everyone, I read something in your journal that kind of bothered me mom. You said something about one of us not being dad's child? Is it me or Zandra? I don't know if you told the girls that part yet, but I just wanted to know if that part of your story was true."

"Well, that is what I wanted to talk to you about. I spoke to your sisters already; did you tell your brother?"

"Yes, I did."

"So again, do you want to walk off so I can talk to you privately or no?"

"Just tell me."

She grabbed my hand and walked me to the guest room.

"Hey Mom, Dell, where are yawl going?" Jr interrupted.

"We will be back."

In the guest room my mother got serious.

"Sit down son."

"O my God! It's me."

"Yes."

My world is spinning; I couldn't breathe. I know I said I didn't want to be a part of Sr, but I was just talking. I didn't think it would come true. But I am a big boy. I got this. I took deep breaths as my mother rubbed my back.

"Sweetheart, are you ok?"

"Yes, Ma, why? Why would you wait fifteen years to tell me something so important?"

"I wanted to say something, but time had slipped by so fast. First, you were born, then the age of three, you turned ten, then thirteen, finally fifteen. I did not know how to tell you at that point. It seemed like you all really love your dad. I was being selfish because you all would have looked at me and hated me. I am so sorry."

"Ma, I would never hate you. I would have been upset, but I wouldn't have hated you. I spoke to Jr, and he said he could see how you would find love somewhere else. You were being abused, for goodness' sake. Also, I had a great life. But now I have so many questions."

"Go ahead, ask me anything."

I cleared my throat. I was nervous and didn't know if I was ready for the answers that I was about to hear.

"Ok. Do you know who my biological father is?"

"Yes, his name is…"

"Wait, mom, do I need to know? Is he a bad person?"

"No, love, he is a very good person, and he's been in your life all of your life."

"Wait, what?"

"Ok, so let me tell you about him. He has been in your life since you have been born. The only reason he was never active in your life was because of me. I didn't want to lose my marriage or my husband. We knew we were wrong for crossing the line, so he agreed with me for him to stay back. So please be mad with me because I forced his hand. However, he stayed as close to you as possible. He is a private chairholder for your school. He donates large amounts of money, and he is a sponsor for your school as well. He's a person that you meet on a regular basis because of his involvement with school. If you would have gotten kicked out when you had that fight, believe me, you would have been able to go back. I know that we are wealthy, but your father is even wealthier."

"Ok, so now who is he?"

"His name is Creon Travis Thompson."

"Hold up, Mom. Do you mean Creon, aka C.T., aka NBA player for the Clippers? The one that always comes to our school and gives pointers on how to ball? The one who finances and teach at the basketball summer camp that I have been going to every year since I can remember? That Creon Travis Thompson?"

"Yes, yes and yes to all of that. I am so sorry, love. He didn't know no other way to be involved."

My mind was racing, and my thoughts were all over the place. I am very close to Creon because he always helped me, always talked to me. The other kids thought that I was his favorite, and I guess I was.

"Isn't he married, Mom?"

"Not anymore. You may see his wife a lot because they co-parent very well. Both are highly involved in their kids' lives but, what happened between him, and I was before he got married. You know he has three other kids by his ex-wife as well. So, you have three smaller siblings."

"I've met them before at camp. They come to the camp every summer and sometimes at school when Creon watches our practice. His son, well, my little brother, I guess, always asks for my help with shooting the ball. He does all of this because of me?"

"Yes."

"I have always wondered why I am so different, where does my attitude come from, why do I look different. It just never seemed like I fit in like everybody else. Mom, you should have told me. I would have kept this between us."

"You would have run to Jr with the quickness telling him how great and better your dad is, so stop frontin."

"Mom, don't ever use that word again." Dell lightly chuckled. Any other time he would have cracked up, but he wasn't in the greatest of moods right now. "And you are right, Mom."

"But all in all, it's still a messed-up situation that you didn't deserve to be in because of two people's mistake. I love you so much, sweetheart, and I want the best for you. I kept secrets from you because you would hate your dad, and I kept secrets from you about your real dad because I didn't want you to hate him for not being around."

"I always felt disconnected. I am somewhat happy with at least knowing that he knows me; he doesn't have a problem being my dad or getting to know me. I can finally start to understand my ways and who I am."

"I hear you. I am glad we talked first. Whenever you have questions, please just come and ask me."

"Does his ex-wife and kids know about me?"

"That is a great question. His ex-wife has always known about you, and his kids know they have a brother, but they don't know who it is. He always brought you around his kids so you all can already be acquainted. He is just waiting on me. And to answer your question before you ask because I know my son, yes, I did make him take a paternity test, and you are his son."

"Ok. I do remember a time when I was showing his son how to shoot, and he said that if he ever would have a brother, he would like for him to be someone like me. Well, that's a relief. I am glad that Creon brought them around me. It won't be so awkward. This is going to be weird. When will I see him on a father/son level now that I know?"

"Another great question, but first, I want to say that it may be weird for you, and I get that. But your biological father has wanted to meet you on this level for years. It was just a sticky situation. This is truly all my fault. I should have told you sooner. Mommy is so so sorry. After everything has calmed down and I know the next steps, I will call Creon and have him come by the house."

"It's ok, Mom, by what I am hearing about the things dad took you through, I am old enough to kind of understand the position you were in. I had a good dad and great mom, so I didn't miss out on anything. I still have time, I guess. Will Sr be at the house when we get home? Because I don't think that I can see him right now. I will probably do something to him."

"I am so proud of you. You are so smart and wise beyond your years. How did I have such a beautiful bright baby." Mom kissed me on my forehead, "And no, your Uncle Zain texted me and told me that your dad is staying with him for a while. Coming to the house wouldn't be smart for the time being."

"Ok, good. So, yes, if we could set that up, mom. Again, I am sorry for what you are going through."

"It's ok. Now that the truth is out, I am happy that everyone is on the same page. We will unravel these issues one at a time until we can get a handle on things. I also want you to know that I….. um…… I am divorcing your dad. I know he is still your dad at the end of the day no matter what he and I have gone through. How do you feel about that?"

"You should. And I got your back. Just because your divorcing dad, that doesn't mean I am. Right?"

Ziola smiled her first genuine smile today.

"Right. You can see him or visit him any time you want."

I can see the relief all over my mother's face. Man, I haven't seen her this happy, ever.

"Come on, mom, I am ready to face the family. I have to tell Jr about this."

"Oh, believe me, the girls have already told him. That's why I wanted to talk to you privately. I can only handle one person at a time with this news."

"Understood." I took my mother's hand in mines and walked with her to the game room. When we entered, everyone was looking at me. I let my mother's hand go, and I walked up to my brother. My siblings all hugged me tight, and I guess they were waiting on me to cry. I looked at them all and lastly looked again at Jr.

"Well, Jr, now I can brag about how my dad is better than yours." Everyone burst out laughing and hugged me again while rubbing my head. I am glad I broke the ice because I was feeling sad inside. I was a little broken but happy at the same time. I can learn about the real me.

Next thing you know, we hear a crack and then a BOOM! All of us ran downstairs, and Noel was already chasing down a female. My brother's car had a huge brick sticking out of the front of it. The side windows were bashed in, and the word WHORE was written in white all over it. At least eight times.

My brother dashed off the porch to catch Noel beating the shit out of some girl. I guess I am not the only one with hands. Noel grabbed her by the hair and was uppercutting the hell out of her. Daaaaaaammmn! Go, Noel. She is so quiet. You would have thought she didn't have a mean bone in her body. Also, I guess my future niece or nephew will be a track star because she should have gone to the Olympics, damn law school, the way she ran that girl down. My brother finally broke up the fight, and now my sisters went after the girl. Whoever this girl is, she came at the right time because my family was mad, angry, and needed someone to take it out on. She did the right thing to piss them off, which was to mess with my sweet whorish brother. My mom even went HAM and got her some fun. Ok, so now, I need to get everybody off this girl. SMH Well, well, well another day full of great drama at the Roze Royss Estates.

Chapter 30

Zander Roze Royss Sr

How did I get here? I allowed my brother to talk me into taking on a life that I have no interest in. I found myself abusing a woman who never deserved an inch of pain. I raised eight kids, all of whom most likely hate me right now. The only people that have my back and is showing a little bit of love towards me is my brother Zain and the love of my life, Beverly. If Ziola takes everything from me, I will still be okay because Beverly opened an account to let me stash money away for when this day would come. Good thing I have a few accounts open in Beverly's name. I have to cover myself.

My life has taken a dangerous turn. It's time for me to make a call that I really did not want to make. Since my brother is not home now, let me get this call out of the way. I found out about this situation a long time ago, but I decided to just leave it alone because I had my own secrets. But now I must make the call.

RING

"Hello."

"Hi Creon, can you meet me at the spot we talked about? It's time."

"Sure, I'll see you in 30."

CLICK

See, Ziola didn't know I knew about Creon, but I did. I drove her to him. He was in love with Ziola, and I couldn't have that. That's why my abuse became worse, but I should have let them be because I didn't really want the relationship to begin with. I just got jealous of what they had, and I knew that I could stop it. Selfish ole me.

RING

"Hello, Monsieur."

"Get the Roze Royss jet ready. I am going on a little trip."

"Si, Senor."

I must get the hell away right now and give myself some time to think. I know that I will be getting a divorce, the kids hate me, so let me get away and get out of everyone's hair for the moment. I'll have Beverly send me some money when I get to the Fairmont Le Chateau Frontenac Hotel in Canada. I need to get pampered to ease this tension. This five-star plush hotel will give me more than enough wine, ladies, and the nature viewing that I need to help me regroup and get back focused. I have to decide on how I am dispersing my money to my kids, including Zandell. He is still my son regardless.

Zain poked his head in the guest room door and scared the shit out of me. You wouldn't believe how we look just alike. Of course, I look better.

"Hey, Bro! I heard you. Where are we going?"

"Damn, you scared the hell of me. And what are you talking about? We are not going nowhere."

"Look, I heard you say, *get the Roze Royss jet ready*. Wherever you are going, I am going too. You need someone to talk to. You are about to be in a whole lotta trouble. Let me help you. We can work together."

"I already have it planned out."

"Ok, well, that's great then! I can go to have fun with you. Man, you need the company, and who better to hang out with you than your own brother. Come on, we haven't enjoyed each other's friendship in a while. Let's go and have fun. It's my fault that you are in this mess anyway, so let me make it up to you. Drinks on me!"

"The drinks are covered."

"Ok, look, look, I'm trying here."

"Fine."

"Yes! Bro time! I'll go pack." Zain darted to his room.

"O Zain?" I hollered.

"Yeah."

"Get packed and go straight to the jet. I have to meet up with someone. I'll meet you in 2 hours. Cool? Two hours Zain, we must get out of here right away."

"Ok. Got you!"

I grabbed my wallet and checked for my cards, ID, and passport. I got everything that I need. Now let me make this stop, then I'm out.

I arrived in record timing. I am not playing about getting out of here quickly, and just as suspected, Creon was sitting in the spot. We met at Lowry Park Zoo in Tampa. The area is filled with families, kids, animals and security. I didn't want something to pop off, and this is the best place because Creon loves the kids. He would never do anything to put kids in harm's way, and just in case he wanted to get stupid, there is security.

I sat on the bench four feet away from him. It was a very secluded area, and he had his bodyguards there. The area where we were, no one could see us. It was the only way to do this. By him being a celebrity and all. We were the only two seated in the area. "It's good to finally meet you, Creon. You're taller than I expected." I smirked. He looked every bit of seven five.

"I see you're shorter than I expected." I saw that coming. Cheap shot. He stared me down with his elbows resting on his knees with his hands were locked and fingers intertwined. He was a good-looking guy. I see why Ziola was head over heels with him. He's big, rich and handsome. I'm not gay. I'm just saying.

"Ok, now that we have the insults out of the way, I wanted to talk to you about my son Zandell."

"Don't you mean my son?" Creon spat.

"No, I meant my son."

We both stood up and faced either other, him, 7'5 and me, 6'0. The bodyguard came and stood in between us.

"Ok, let me say what I have to say. I know you will now be a part of my, um, our son's life. I am just here to say, if you are going to choose to be in his life, please be a part of his life. Don't change your mind about it."

"I never have nor will I ever. I have always been here for him mentally and physically. I have and will continue to train him, be his guide and support him always. Don't tell me how to be a father. I would have already been in his life if it wasn't for you and Ziola. But I can understand where Zi came from, but you, never. If it wasn't for Ziola, I would have never known our son."

"Ok, I get it, and I am innocent in this. I didn't know that she stepped out on me until years later."

"Look, I don't care. You knew that Zandell was not your son, and I know you told Ziola not to let him see me, but for fifteen years I have been in his life, so good try. I am good and you can miss me with that be-a-good-father talk. You are the one that need the daddy talk and the know-how-to-treat-your-woman talk too. I know what you did to Ziola. If she had allowed me to be her man, you would be dead right now. This convo is over." He started to walk off, and I had to say the hardest thing ever in my life.

"A yo, Creon!"

"What?"

"Don't let him grow up to be like me. Just take care of him, please. I love him so much."

"Now, that is something I can do. And all jokes aside, I know you love him and in saying that I am out. This crowd is about to get thick. I got him, don't worry." He walked off, and that was that.

Now I got to get to Canada because Florida is getting hotter than a Bitch around here. I walked quickly to my corvette and hopped in. I mashed the gas and got the hell out of there and headed to the jet.

RING

"Hello sweetheart are you ok?"

"Beverly, I am getting out of town for a while. I need some money. But I'll call you with the details. Please don't tell anyone but I am going to Canada."

Chapter 31

ZADA ROZE ROYSS

I received a weird text from my dad telling me to handle all the business affairs as he will be out of town for a while to clear his head. I bet. He is under a lot of heat here at the mansion. Mom is being a thorn in his behind, and no one is talking to him. Our family secrets are just spilling out like a running faucet. Well, now I see where I get it from. I am headed to my appointment to talk to Noel about my divorce. Will I have to pay my husband money per month, or will he have to pay me? With me being pregnant and all, I will probably have to pay him. Hopefully, she can get around that.

Also, Raphael is not playing. I know he can take care of me, but I have always taken care of myself. I don't ever want to put myself in a situation where there is another soul that has any financial, mental or physical control over me. You see how that turned out for my mother. I am just at a loss here, but I want out of this god-forsaken marriage.

I pulled up to this beautiful building and let the valet park my car. As I strolled through looking at the beautiful flowers and the people walking about, I thought about my life and how happy I am to be running my father's real-estate company. I'll be owning it soon. My father will be retiring, especially now that he has so much going on. I know he has some money stashed and he is ready to live his life how he wants. Especially, since he's lived someone else's life. I remember the love he had for my mom; I saw it in his eyes. Maybe it was a lie, but there was something there. Oh well, it is surely gone now.

I stepped off the elevator to approach the secretary, but Noel was already waiting there for me.

"Hey, Love, let's go to my office."

I followed her, and I can honestly say, my brother wised up and embraced this stella of a woman. Not only is she an attorney, but she has a sense of humor, smart, wife material, has some spunk, and she's not scared to throw some hands.

I looked around her office, and it spoke of the woman that I knew. The office was decorated with deep rich black wood, very elegant with her black-on-black oak desk. She had a picture of her and my brother inside one of her built-in shelves. Her window stood from the floor all the way up to the ceiling, where you can see all downtown Tampa. It was an amazing view. This is an office where you can have peace and tranquility.

Noel is expensive too. To hire her, you have to pay a 10-thousand-dollar fee for the retainer alone. She is a shark in the courtroom. I am glad she is on my team, and this is free for me. Lol, I can afford it a hundred times over, but it feels good when you know people in high places. Her built-in mini bar had assortments of liquor and wine. This has to be for her clients.

"So, Zada, how is it going? How can I help you?" she asked once we'd sat down.

"You tell me. I have been married for a while now, and it has not been good. We have not slept with each other in over a year. We sleep in separate rooms and everything. I want to just be fair and walk away, but he has threatened me about taking everything I got. We got married in Hawaii, so the infidelity laws apply."

"Ok, so has he committed adultery that you know of?"

"Honestly, I don't know. I hired a private investigator, but they came up with nothing. He wasn't a good PI, if I say so myself. It seemed like he just wanted money. I know that Alex is hiding something. I can't run behind him playing detective because I run my real-estate company. My father has left me in charge of everything for a while. Also, I am pregnant."

"Ok, wait. So, if you are pregnant and you haven't slept with your husband within that last year, you are pregnant by someone else, which means you have committed adultery and Alex can go as far as suing your child's father. Who may I ask are you pregnant by?

"Raphael Lovechild aka Ca$h. Yes, he is rich, but Raphael does not care. However, I do not want him to get sued."

"Well, per Hawaii's marriage laws, Alex can sue. But what I will do is get my PI on Alex. He's one of the greatest PI's I know. I am not saying Alex is cheating, but it would break you guys even if he is. Just give me some time to investigate it and I'll let you know if there is something or nothing. Cool?"

"Thank you, Noel, and yes, that is cool."

"Don't worry. Everything will be fine. I got you." Her smile was so warming. I see why my brother is going crazy over this woman.

"Oh yes, Noel, my brother knows nothing about nothing, me having issues in my marriage, me dealing with another man and of course the pregnancy. Please don't tell him. He will know in due time."

"Oh yes what we discuss is confidential. I would never. I take my oath seriously."

"Ok. I am happy you are back in the family, Noel. My brother is very lucky."

She smiled at me. "I am lucky, too, Zada. See you soon, and I'll be in touch."

"Ok. Bye."

I walked out of her office feeling brand new. I finally took my first step to getting out of this ridiculous, stupid and crazy marriage. I can't wait to tell Raphael. I needed to do this because he would pull up to the crib like a madman!

Before I went back to the estate, I am going to see Raphael.

RING

"Hello, beautiful."

"Hi, handsome. What are you doing?"

"In Miami about to do this video shoot. Were you trying to stop by?"

"Yes, but your hours away."

"I can fly you here, and we can make a week of it."

"No, babe, it's ok. My dad left for a little while and I have to run things for a bit, but I would have definitely taken you up on your offer if he was here. I'll be working a lot in the next month or so. You'll be gone for a week?"

"Yes, I was going to call you, but things moved so fast. My management team be on it. You know, if you ever need me, it doesn't matter what I am doing or where I am. I'll always get to you or get you to me. Are you ok? How is the baby, any kicking yet? I can't wait to feel the baby kick."

"Yes, I am doing great. No kicking yet. I am only 8 weeks." I giggled. "I am happy that you are excited."

"Of course, I am excited. I've always wanted to be a father, but I had to wait for the right time and the right woman, and since I have both, I am elated! We will have at least 3 kids, so get ready lil momma."

"Hahaha, ok, whatever you say. I spoke to my lawyer today, and she is working on everything."

"Oh, word?"

"Word." I laughed again.

"That's what I'm talking about! I can't wait to shout to the world who my lady is, and Ca$h is about to have a baby!!!"

"I bet."

"Did she say what he can sue me for?"

"No, she just said she would be checking to see if he is straight or not on his end. Then we can go from there. We will be able to just go our separate ways, but if not, then he can sue for a lot. I am so sorry about this. I should have left and then started this relationship. I don't want you to go through this."

"Listen, you and your soon-to-be ex-husband were already at the end of your ropes. You are not the only one at fault. I allowed it too. I could have walked away, but I didn't, Ma. Don't worry. Everything will work out. You were a great wife and a phenomenal mother. He changed, not you. Remember that. You wouldn't have had to step out if he was taking care of you and home. So, I regret nothing. Do you hear me? Nothing."

"I hear you."

I heard someone in the background calling for him. I started to feel sad. I was loving our moment.

"Ok, that's my queue. They're calling yo boy. I'll call you later to check on you, ok? Everything will be fine. No worries. I got you."

"Ok, I'll talk to you later."

"Zanny, don't sound sad. Stop it. Our time will come. You know I love you, right?"

"Yes, I love you too." He must have put his hand over the phone because I heard him shout out in a muffled tone. He got mad with the person in the background.

"Hold on muthafucka. I got my future wife on the phone. Hello, Red?"

"Yes, I'm here. I'll let you get back to work. Kisses to your lips."

"Kisses back Ma."

CLICK

I cried because I hated being in this situation. I should have left my husband a long time ago. We honestly just married for status purposes. We thought that we could make it work, but I found out later that his father knew their real-estate company was failing, so he tried to get his son connected with a family that could hold him down for life. He could have had that life, but after I didn't have a son, he started treating me like dirt. I remember when he had gotten so mad with me one time. My daughter couldn't sleep because she was teething. He was yelling at me to shut her up.

"Shut her the hell up. I'm trying to sleep in this bitch."

"I can't. Her gums are hurting her. She is teething, Alex. I'll go into the other room then."

"No, leave her ass in her room and let her cry. She will fall asleep eventually. Lay yo ass back down."

"Wait, I am not leaving my baby to cry. You're crazy! I am going to put more Orajel on her gums and rock her to sleep."

I got up after ten minutes of rocking her to sleep and laid her in her bassinette right by my side. When I turned around to fix my pillow, Alex was sitting up. He raised his hand and back slapped the hell out of me. He hit me so hard that I fell off the bed. I'm glad the bassinette wasn't too close, or I would have fallen on the baby.

I cried instantly. "What the fuck did you do that for?"

"Because when I tell you to do something, you better fucking do it. Don't goddamn talk back to me." And he turned away to go back to sleep.

Did I just walk in the twilight zone? Did this nigga just hit me? Nope, not in this lifetime!! I grabbed whatever was in my view that was hard, which was my clock off my nightstand. I jumped on his ass, and in the way I jumped on him, I was straddling his back. I wailed on his punk ass with that hard clock. I was swinging and hitting him in the back of his head, ears, everywhere. The baby woke up and started crying because she was cussing him out with me.

"Don't.... You.... Ever.... Put... yo... damn.... Hands.... On .... Me...... again.... You... low.... life...broke...ass.....Son... Of......A......Bitch......I... will.... Kill...... you.... Agggggghhhhhhh!"

I went Tina Turner on his ass. He didn't know what hit him. My daughter was 6 months old at the time. That was the last night that I got hit by him, the last night I laid in the bed with him, and that was the last night I felt anything for him.

Three days later, time is flying by, and I am so happy because I can't wait to see Raphael. I miss him. I have been sick, throwing up every morning like clockwork. My first pregnancy was nice and easy-going. This is horrible. I am happy that I am in my own room nowadays. Alex would hear me if we were in the same bed. Also, good thing my daughter sleeps like a true tired baby.

Right now, I am sitting in my office, and it's 6:30 pm. I am so sick, tired and hungry, but I am scared to eat anything. Working like a dog, I closed five houses today. I will be leaving around 7 pm and not staying for no one. I heard the doorbell chime, and I was looking at the door like nobody else is coming in here, but it was Noel. I got up to unlock the door.

"Hey Noel, you just caught me before leaving. I closed on five houses today, and I am taking tomorrow off. I am sick like crazy and so tired. What's up, though? Is my brother, ok? You good?"

"Awwwwww, I am so sorry. Being pregnant has got to be a full-time job."

"Oh yes, it is, especially when you are sick. I'm scared to eat because it hurts so bad. I can't wait until this sickness passes."

Yeah, I hear you. Where is your mom, and when is your dad coming back? You need a break for a couple of days."

"Well, my mom is coming to the office tomorrow, finally. We have to close some more houses, so she is going to do it. My dad is gone until further notice. I don't know when he is coming back. I don't blame him; I'd be scared too. So, what brings you by? Why didn't you just come to the house?"

" Well, I came here to talk to you about something, and I didn't know if Alex was home."

"Oh, right, yeah, he is." She walked to the sofa in my office and patted the empty space next to her, with her soft French manicured nails. She had a manila folder resting on her lap. She had a serious look on her face that scared me a bit.

I got up from my desk and gently sat by Noel.

"Zada, I had Raphael and Alex checked out for you. And I have some information that you will want to know."

My heart skipped a beat because I didn't know she was going to look into Raphael too. If Raphael is cheating or has another life, I think I would die right here on the spot.

"I didn't know you were going to look into Raphael, Noel. I didn't tell you to do that. Why did you?"

"Because before we go down this road, I want to make sure that you are being treated like you deserve. I have heard your story with your husband, and I wanted to see if Ca$h was really in it with you because if not, we would have to work on child support. I wanted to kill two stones in one so you can truly calm your nerves. Ca$h is in Miami on a video shoot, and he is working hard. He does party, though, and the ladies love him, but my PI says that he hasn't had anyone in his room. All though a naked woman was in there when he arrived the first night. Relax! He had her kicked out." She started laughing because of the look on my face. "Your man is clean and faithful."

"Oh, my goodness, that is a relief. I would have killed him. Literally. Ok, so that is good news. What else?"

"Well, do you know this woman?" Noel passed me a picture of an attractive lady wearing an all-white business suit. Her hair was tied up in a tight neat bun to the back with a butterscotch-colored briefcase in her hand. She was brown skin with a straight face. She looked like she was all about her business. Her eyes were full of life like she had it all together."

"Wait a minute. I know who exactly this is. This is Cynthia Black, my best friend from growing up. We were friends since the age of ten. We went our separate ways after college. She moved to Utah and got married, and had two children, from what I was told. She stopped answering my calls and emails. I just left her alone because it was obvious that she didn't want to be bothered with me anymore. What does she have to do with anything?"

"She is married and has two kids. She is also a lawyer as well and her father is now a judge. She is well off."

"Ok, so Noel, why are we talking about her?"

"Does Alex go to Utah a lot?"

"All the time, his father's main realty office and his board of realtors are located there. In fact, he has said he ran into her a few times, but she just ignores him like he doesn't exist, like we didn't all go to college together and were the best of friends. Why?"

"Ok, here are the rest of the pictures that I have."

I continued to look on as she passed me picture after picture. I saw Cynthia and Alex playing with the kids together, and they were at events with the kids. I saw them at dinner together, but just the two of them and no one else.

She then gave me a picture of a marriage certificate with Alexander and Cynthia Black-Picrson. And the second picture with both children's birth certificates with his name as the father. The little boy is six, and the girl is five. My daughter is 2. What the fuck?

"Woooooo, please break this down to me. This is a lot right now coming at me at once. Please explain slowly and thoroughly. Where did you get these pictures from? Alex is here right now."

"My PI went to all social media platforms and got these pictures. He also has connections in pretty much every state. She has a very private life because of her father and has very few friends. So, no one would have known about you and her being married to the same man. Your circles are different. You don't know this, but Alex is not broke. His real-estate company has Utah on lock. So, let me break this down to you like you said."

"Your husband is legally married to Cynthia. In UTAH, bigamy is allowed, so when he married you, he didn't see anything wrong with it. I am quite sure Cynthia knows about you, and she may be ok with all of this, though I can't be sure. The two children are his. Cynthia and Alex hooked up in college when you were still involved with him. Alex graduated before you two, but she never said anything about the relationship, of course."

"Wait. How do you know all of this?"

"I have a reliable source."

With an almost teary and shaky voice, "Ok, go on."

"Ok, Zada, you are not legally married. You do not have to get a divorce because his marriage to Cynthia automatically voids yours. I'll just have to get him for child support. If you want to press charges, I can do that because bigamy is not allowed in Florida. However, that is up to you. Also, I know someone who can just wipe your slate clean, and no one will have to know that there ever was a marriage on paper. If you want him to go to jail, just say the word, and I will make it happen. What he did was illegal. He could get up to five years in prison for this. I'll just have to work my magic to get you off the books showing you two are not married, or like I said, let the marriage show and have him arrested."

I didn't know what to say because I have been living a lie. He stole everything from me. I could have taken my time finding someone to love me for me, not be someone's punching bag or sex toy. He hated me and didn't want me. Why would he do this? What was the point? Holy Shit, my money, he can't take it.

"Zada this is a lot right now. I'll leave these pictures with you. I wouldn't advise you to address him on this by yourself. You should have your brother or someone there, so you don't react in a bad way, and I have to get you out of jail. I know this is hard, but please do not address him without anyone around. I can have him removed from the house if you like. We can talk about child support later. Let me ask you, do you want full custody?"

The look I gave her said it all.

"Ok, I will start drafting papers, and I will let you know what you will be getting per month. You and your kids and your kid's kids will not have to work ever. You have a lot of money circulating back to you, and after this divorce, you will want for nothing. It's sad but true. I am so sorry about this, Zada. I know you didn't expect this."

"No, I didn't," I said in a hushed tone. Raphael would be pissed that Alex used me like that. He might rip Alex apart. Oh no. This is a mess. I can't believe I am living my mother's life. Wait until she hears this bullshit.

Chapter 32

ZIOLA ROZE ROYSS

RING

"Hello."

"Hi Creon, this is…"

"I know, my Zi. How are you?"

"I am great. How are you?"

"I am always good. Especially now that I hear your voice."

"How sweet. Um, it's about that time that you and Zandell meet on a father-son level. He knows."

"Yeah, I kind of figured that when Zander called me for a meet up."

"He did what?" Creon told me all about the visit and how they almost came to blows. Zander has some nerve. But I have some nerve too, because I should have never stepped outside of our marriage, regardless of how my husband treated me.

"I want you to know, your husband knew for years. You didn't know, but he called me right after you had Zander, and he told me to stay away from you and the baby. This was after you and

I decided that I can be involved in my own way. So that is why I didn't go over there to crack that nigga's neck, but yes, he did call me. So, I am sorry that it had to come to Zandell finding out the truth so late. I am more than happy to meet with him and sit down to talk things out. Ziola, I will be telling him the truth no matter how bad it may sound. He needs to know."

"That is fine. I told him everything anyway, but I am sure you have more to tell him."

"I do. How are you holding up with all of this?"

"I'm ok. I am scared, nervous, and happy all at once. I am relieved that the truth is out. Even though I could not stand my husband and didn't care about cheating on him, I feel bad for my son. He always felt different from the rest of his siblings. I am happy that he can get all his questions answered."

"Fasho. I am also going to tell him you are and still is the love of my life."

"Don't do that, Creon."

"Seriously, I am. I do not want my son thinking that I never loved his mother or that what we had was just a booty call. That is not the truth. I told you, I am telling him everything. My ex-wife even knows that if it wasn't for you, wanting to work it out with your husband, she and I would have never even made it to the alter. You would have had my other three kids. We would have had four kids plus your babies. Hahaha, Dead ass."

"I still love you too, but I am not going down that road right now. Especially going through this divorce, it's going to take a toll on me. I have to handle this first and get my stuff in line."

"Divorce!!! Awwww man! You just lifted my spirits! So, I can start working on you to be mine again! I am getting the love of my life back and my son all wrapped into one!!!!! This is my lucky day. I have to call all of my chicks and tell them it's over!"

I was cracking up because Creon is so funny, but I knew he was serious with what he was saying. Me and Creon were tighter than tight. Our affair lasted for three years, but it got serious when I got pregnant. I had to put on a front with my husband, but my heart was elsewhere.

"Really cute, Creon and I can't with you. I have to focus on my divorce like I said and get my affairs in order. I'm focusing on taking care of myself and my kids."

"Believe me, you and your kids will get taken care of. You are a package, and I am ready to get my delivery."

"That is so corny. Hahahahaha"

"Naw, but I'll give you your space to handle your business, but I am about to pursue you, so get ready. But I will be telling our son the truth about how I felt and how I feel about you. So, I am just preparing you. Anyway, just call me and let me know when I can see him. He can come to my place if that's ok with you?"

"Ok, I'll talk to him and see where his head is, and I'll get back to you. Cool?"

"Cool. It was a pleasure talking to you Ms. Ziola."

"Yes, it was. Talk to you soon.'

"Ok, now I have to start calling these chicks."

"Hahahaha, Bye boy."

"Bye."

I am in trouble. Creon always did something to me. That's why I had to break it off when I became pregnant. I had a plan to leave my husband and everything, but I just couldn't do that to my kids. I just cut him off and let him be a dad to his son from afar. Well, one thing is for sure, I have been fell out of love with Sr a long time ago, so my heart is wide open, but this time, I am waiting until I am divorced before I carry on with any man. I want it to start out right so it can continue to be right.

Chapter 33

ZADA ROZE ROYSS

Really. Is this what my life has turned into? A ball of a fucking mess. My husband, no, my crabby-fuck-ass-husband has a whole fucking family on the side. I am sitting here cooking, cleaning, taking care of our daughter and being treated like shit. I never fully loved Alex one hundred percent, but I felt like I could grow to love him and cherish him. He changed after I had a daughter instead of a son. How could he treat me like shit when he had what he wanted on the side? You see, men are so damn stupid. He could have treated me with the utmost respect, could have had two lives, and I would not have looked into anything. He would have been living the life without me knowing it. So stupid.

I would have been blind and thought that my husband is the shit, but men can't do that. They have to change on a bitch. They have to stay out all night on a bitch, they get sloppy on a bitch, they start to smell their own ass on a bitch. Not women, no, not women. We will have another nigga in our closet for years, before our main man finds out and that's if he does! What the fuck! He could have been honest with me, and we could have worked something out privately, quietly and went our separate ways.

But noooooo not Mr. Fast Ass. Oh no. Well, I am walking away, and I want him served in UTAH, where him and his bitch lives. I can't believe my own old best friend. She always wanted everything I had. Always. She used to wear my clothes when I went home for the holidays. I would curse that bitch out for using my shit. We fell out right before we graduated college. We got into a big argument.

"Cynthia, why in the fuck do you keep wearing my shit? I told you that after that time you bled in my five-hundred-dollar dress, and put that shit back in my damn closet instead of cleaning that shit, you couldn't wear my shit anymore. So why are you still wearing my shit?"

"I didn't wear yo shit."

"Yes, you did because this dress is brand new bitch, and it smells like musk. What the fuck!"

"I don't know what you are talking about. So, take your anger out on somebody else. It sounds like Alex need to tap that ass so you can relieve some stress. Hahaha."

"Don't try to turn this around. You don't respect my things, and if you touch something else, I'm going to put my foot in yo ass. Yo daddy makes enough money to buy you your own shit."

"I dare you."

"What?" Did this bitch try me!

"Yeah, that's right. I dare you, yup, I wore yo shit. I didn't feel like going shopping, so I wore it. What you gon do about it?"

Before you knew it, I had that bitch's hair in my fist and started wailing on her ass. I was upper cutting the shit out of her. I slung her ass on the floor and fucked her up. Our next-door dorm mates heard commotion, so she opened the door to see what was going on and yelled fight. Two other dorm mates came over and broke us up.

"I'mma kill you. You messed up my hair."

"Fuck you. I told you not to wear my shit! Stay the hell outta my damn closet skank."

"I am going to sue you for assault."

See, way back then, that bitch had an attorney's mindset.

"Do it! I dare you! Hahahahahaha." Her ass doesn't have more money than me. She got life fucked up.

We were asked to see the principal, but because we were graduating next week, she let it slide. Our asses were out of there anyway.

I had a hot temper in college. Your risk-taking attitude when your young is daring and reckless. My attitude went away a long time ago. After college, Alex and I started our careers and then got married because our families' social group thought it was for the best. In a way, Alex forced me to be able to cheat and forced me to be an adulterer. I hate him for that. Why couldn't he just live his life with Cynthia and leave me alone. I feel hurt and confused.

Well, I guess my daughter and I will be well off after this divorce or walk away. Smh. That's a good thing. I'll have to talk to Raphael, so I know what we have is solid. I wish I could have learned all of this about Alex before the baby. I would have walked away and moved on with my life, but it didn't happen that way. Now, I have to deal with the cards with how they are laid out before me. I must take accountability for my actions, but you better believe that Alex will too.

After hearing this devastating news, I walked in the house, and as usual, I was greeted with bullshit.

"Hey, where have you been? I have to get to the airport and head out to Utah! You know I have an important meeting tomorrow. Here, take her."

He shook me out of the trance that I was in and shoved Alexis in my arms. She was crying so bad. I was a little confused because he never acted like this toward our daughter. I play about a lot of things, but I don't play about my baby. Now, messing with my baby will bring out the college Zada.

"Don't you dare handle my baby like that. I don't give a shit about what you need to do or where you need to be. Don't you fucking toss my daughter to me like that. If I would have dropped her because of your negligence…"

"What? What would you have done? Huh? Huh, Zada? Hurt me? Hahaha. You ain't gon do shit but stand there and shut the fuck up. I can do what the fuck I want to. Now, if you don't mind, I have a fucking flight to catch."

That muthafucka walked off. I envision myself picking up my vase that was in my peripheral vision and crashing that shit against his fucking skull.

I was so mad, but the idea that came to mind relaxed me. I just stood there watching him grab one small suitcase and head out the door. I just looked at him with hatred and disgust in my eyes. He was happy with how he talked to me in front of our daughter. He has no regard for me whatsoever.

When he opened the door to leave, he took one last look at me.

"I should have never married you; you are such a waste of my time. I'll see you when I get back, unfortunately." And slammed the door shut. Now, I don't know if it was my hormones or if his words really hurt me, but I boo woo cried right along with my baby girl.

RING

"Hello, Zay, what's up?"

I called Zaniyah because I needed a babysitter for Alexis. I had some important business to handle.

"Hey, you, how is it going? School and all." I tried so hard not to let her hear that I had just been boo hoo crying a minute ago.

"Oh, it's going great. My grades are always stellar as usual, and parties are live. What's up with you? How are you holding up?"

"I am not. I need a favor. What will you be doing for the next couple of days?"

"Nothing really, and if I had something going on, I can always adjust my schedule. My classes are completed until next school year. However, I am thinking about taking a class during the summer so I can finish early. I am getting sick of school. Why, what's up?

"Well, I need a babysitter. I need to handle some business, and I can't do it with Alexis. If my business is handled, I should be back by tomorrow night. Can you, do it?"

"I sure can, let me grab some things, and I'll be over there in a jiffy. Can I have a friend over?"

"Yes, but no screwing in my damn house Zaniyah, I am not playing. Remember what happened last time."

"Yes, I know. It's a girl. We are talking about entrepreneurship ideas, and what better place to talk about that than your big mansion. It will motivate us."

Her laugh was so young with energy, no worries, vibrate and just pure. I wish I felt like that right now.

"Ok, that's fine. Thank you, Sis."

"No problem, why do I get the feeling that this is not a business trip?"

"It is, and I'll tell you all about it when I get back. Ok?"

"Oooook. On my way."

RING

"Hello, this is Zada Roze Royss-Pierson. Please get the Roze Royss jet ready for departure."

"Of course, Mrs. Roze Royss-Pierson. And where are we headed tonight?"

"UTAH."

Chapter 34

ZANDELL ROZE ROYSS

As I am looking out of the window, I see such a beautiful day. The skies are perfect with its touch of crystal blue. There were hints of soft white clouds springling across the sky, which made my heart swell.

My mom shook me out of my trance. "Zandell, are you ready?"

"I'm coming, mom."

We are going to Creon's home, and I am pretty geeked up about it, but, at the same time, I'm also nervous. I have seen this man a million times. Why am I tripping? I changed my clothes like a runway male model. Smh

I wore navy blue khaki shorts with my white, red, and navy-blue polo. I had on my all-white air force ones, and my hair cut was waved up perfectly after my daily ritual of brushing 150 times. Now I know where I get these waves from.

My dad meaning Sr, is balled and wear it well but he never had waves like this, Jr don't either. He has a Caesar fade and he had to work hard to get them waves. He brushes 150 times a day just like me. That's who I get it from. Sr didn't pass that down to us.

I am looking dapper than ever. I just want to make a great impression as his son when he sees me in this way for the first time. My 6-foot 6-inch height is crazy. I have grown so much since all of this has happened. It is like my body is happy with knowing Creon is my dad. My mom told me until I am sixteen, I will still possibly grow. I'll be sixteen in a month, so I guess I am at my highest height. I am taller than everyone in my family. Period. Now I know where I am getting it all from.

We are driving, and I am shaking my leg like crazy because I don't know what else to do. My mother puts her warm, delicate hand on my knee to calm my nerves.

"You look so handsome; I love what you have on." I can tell that my mom is trying to break the ice, but it's not working.

"So Zandell, how are you feeling?" she pressed when I didn't reply.

I sigh. "I am all over the place. I am nervous and happy all at once. It's confusing. I don't understand it. I have seen Creon a thousand times. I have never felt like this before, even when I knew I was meeting a big-time celebrity."

"Well, you are meeting Creon as your dad for the first time. This is not about sports, a camp or hanging out. This is something a bit more serious."

"A bit?"

"Ok, something more serious. It's ok to be nervous, and I am sure he is nervous too. Just take a deep breath and relax. Mommy will be with you the whole time. If you are not comfortable, just shoot me a sign, and I will get you up and out of there. Ok?"

"Ok, Mom. Thanks."

"You're welcome, love."

"Will his kids be there?"

"Honestly, sweetheart, I do not know how this will go, but we will take it one step at a time. I will be there for it all unless you tell me that you are good and don't need me."

"Mom, I'll always need you. Thanks for being here with me."

"Of course, no doubt!"

"Mom, don't ever say that again." We shared a wholesome laugh.

"One thing I can say, that may hopefully make you feel better, is that Creon is excited to see you too. He's always wanted to be a-part of your life and I am so sorry that I did this to the both of you. I really am." My mom held hand.

"Mom, I get it. You are worried about me, but I will be fine. What about you? How are you holding up? What are you thinking about?"

"Hahaha, ok my growing man. Right now, I am thinking about you with wanting this scary experience to be a joyous one. When I am done with this situation, then I can think about me. So, one thing at a time. That's how people go into a deep depression, they think about everything all at once instead of resolving their issues one by one. That's the best way to handle anything that comes your way."

"Great lesson mom. Hahahaha."

"We are here."

※

When we made a right on this deserted street, there was a black iron gate with an intercom on the left side. The gate was tall, with a light tan wall holding it up. My mom punched in a code. Hmmm, how did she know the code? Are they that close?

We continued to drive down a winding road where you couldn't see nothing but trees. There were peach trees, orange trees and everything you can imagine. It was a beautiful sight. This will be a part of my life. Wow. The property was beautiful but not more beautiful than what was up ahead. I finally was able to see the home that Creon lived in. The trees begin to disappear. We were now on a circular road to the house.

I can't believe it. I started to shake my leg again, but my mom put her hand back on my knee. This house looked amazing. It's a modern contemporary home that was light tan with the walls made of rocks. You can see straight through the house because the windows were tall with thick glass. The house was lit up with lights on in every room. It looked like a gigantic cabin but with big glass windows. I saw a figure upstairs, and as we came to a stop; I saw that it was Creon. He walked away from the window to greet us, I guess. And I was right. He opened a tall door that looked like bigfoot could easily walkthrough. That's when I froze, my palms started to get sweaty, and I was starting to have a hard time breathing. I didn't move.

My mother threw up her forefinger to Creon, and he nodded. And she turned to me.

"Hey, relax. Zandell Roze Royss, you listen to me. I know that this is new, difficult, and scary. I get it. But I want you to know that this is happening and the young man I raised you to be can overcome any obstacles that come his way. You are smart, you are brave, you are great, and you are my son. I will be with you every step of the way, and I promise you everything will be ok."

I still didn't move.

"Ok, so let's treat this like basketball. Think of how the material of a ball feels in your hands and how great of a player you are. Think of your fans yelling your name." Ziola cupped her mouth with her hands as if she was the crowd at a basketball game. "Zandell, Zandell, Zandell."

Zandell started to smile.

Ziola continued. "You are about to make your famous three pointer and you go for the shot while everyone looks on and BOOM! Your three pointer is the point that wins the game!"

I started to laugh because I was feeling so much better. My mom is the best and she knew exactly how to relax me. She does it every time.

"Ok, mom, I'm good now."

"Hey, one more thing, I don't care who it is. I don't want you to ever be scared or nervous to see or meet anybody because you are Zandell Roze Royss. Always remember it is an honor for them to meet you, for them to be in your presence, for them to be in your life, and be a part of you, not the other way around. Do you hear me?"

"Yes, Ma'am, I do. Ok, let's do this."

"Ok, let's do this."

We got out of her white Lexus LX-570 and walked up to the massive door. I stuck my hand out to shake Creon's hand, and in return, he grabbed my hand and pulled me in for the biggest bear hug I have ever had. I felt a lot better. My headache went away, my nervousness faded, and my anxiety dissipated. I felt at home.

Creon walked us to the family room to have a seat.

"Would you like something to eat? I made Cuban sandwiches with all the fixings. Your mom said that Cubans are your favorite. I am so happy because I can make a mean Cuban."

I nodded my head. "Yeah, that would be great. I am hungry."

Ziola chimed in.

"Yes, that would be great."

"Ok, I'll go and grab that, and both of you can relax. Be right back."

He ran off while my mom and I sat on a soft plush sofa. His house was immaculate. It was a baller's dream. He had light gray, black, white and silver furniture. It looked so athletic and cool. He has a black and gray basketball on a mantel with his name and year on it. It looked like an eighty-inch TV in the family room along with a huge rocked-out fireplace. Wow, wow, wee!!!

"Ok, this is for you, Ziola, and this is for you, Zandell. I hope you like it."

"I am sure I will." My mom spoke to break the silence because Creon was just staring at me, and I was staring at him.

"Ok, men, I am going to eat my sandwich in the kitchen to give you guys some space. Zandell, are you ok with that, or do you want me to sit with you?"

"No, I am good, mom. Thanks."

"Of course, sweetheart." She kissed me on my forehead and walked out.

"We look alike. I never really noticed that before. My teammates would always say that we looked like father and son. Now I see where I get everything from."

He smiled at me.

"Your mother told me that she told you everything, so I will be honest with you as well. I am not trying to justify anything your mother and I did. It was wrong, and I should have never pursued your mother, knowing her situation. I am so sorry that I did that. I am sorry that I kept this from you as well. It was just a messy situation, and I didn't want to tear your mother's marriage apart."

"But you did by having me. Now my father has one less son."

"And you are so right, Zandell. I messed up, and I can't do anything to change that but to say that I am so sorry that you were caught in the middle, when you did not ask for this."

I just look at the man that created me. This is my real father.

"I am a little upset that this has happened, but I am also relieved because I always had a feeling of disconnect. Not from my mother, but from my dad. He always tried too hard to be there, and sometimes he would act like I didn't exist. Honestly, you played a bigger role in my life than him. My father never played basketball with me. My mom was the first one to put a ball in my hand. She was the one to tell me to try out for the team. Was that you talking through her to me?" His look gave it away.

"Yes, Zandell. I saw that you had the height, and I just asked your mom to do certain things to see if basketball would be in your future. If it wasn't, we were going to find what you were good at and push that greatness in you. Basketball just worked out. Hell, your better than me."

I smiled because I am great on the court, I mean for real for real. Lol

※

"I wish I could have been there more. Your mother and I agreed that it would be best for me to be active from afar. It killed me to see you being raised without me there day to day. I don't like that you had to find out this way, and I don't like that this has happened to you. However, I am so happy that it is out there, and you finally know about it. If you are ok with me being in your life, I would be honored to get to know you, get to love you, which I already do." We laughed, "I want to get to teach you, play with you, grow with it, be there with you through it all. That would make me the happiest man alive. I know this is a lot, and I am fine with you taking your time with this if need be. Hell, if you feel like this is not what you want, I will respect that too. So, what do you say? Can we work on us? Father and son?"

Wow, wow, wow. Sr never ever had a heart-felt conversation with me like this.

"I would like to work on us too. I am ready. No time better than the present."

Creon stood up and bear-hugged me again. I wonder if this will be a regular thing. So, I need to put my foot down now. Once we got finishing hugging, I stood my ground. But before I could get a word out, my mother started yelling!

"Yes!! About time!!" She came out of the kitchen and started hugging both of us. This is ridiculous.

"Ok, ok, ok, ma."

"Sorry, I am just so happy that this secret is out and in the open."

"Ok Creon, I have something to say before we go any further."

"Ok."

"I know that this is a long time coming for you and your happy, and I am too. But I am not a hugging type of person. We can dap and shake hands like we used to do. Hug me only when you feel I need it. No disrespect."

My mom and Creon bust out laughing. I guess what I said was the funniest thing, but I am dead serious. Smh

"None taken. I can stop hugging you for now, but I will have to do that every now and then. I am just happy, that's all."

"Ok, that fine but not all the time, though."

RING

"Yes, you guys can come in the house now. See you soon."

"Who was that?" I asked.

"That was your brother and sisters. I told them to play in the treehouse outback. They already know about you. They are ecstatic. Especially CJ, he wants to pick your brain on big brother stuff. Wow, I didn't ask. Are you ok with this? My bad Zan."

We heard a commotion and all of us turned our heads to the back of the house, and I saw three little kids running toward me with their arms out.

I shot him a look. "I guess I am."

Omg! More hugs? I guess it's ok. These little hugs, I am ok with.

Chapter 35

Zada Roze Royss

As I sit in my rental car, with my eyes watching a mini-mansion in Draper, UTAH; I wondered how I got to the point of doing a steak out. I had to see this for myself. Just when I was about to dose off, I saw a pearl Lexus back out of the garage. I was on the alert then; I didn't start my car until the car drove off. I turned my car lights on and followed the Lexus to its destination. It was about 7:45pm. I followed the LX to a restaurant called Carver's Steak and Seafood. The car was about three to four spaces down from me. I needed to see it; I had to see it.

Just like hocus-pocus, I saw the driver's door start to open, and Alex got out. I looked on in bewilderment. My husband, I mean my boyfriend, looked happier than I had ever seen him. I couldn't believe how alive and healthy he looked. He was dressed nice and neat with a fresh haircut. He stood with his back straight like he was on top of the world.

The back door on his side opened, and sure enough, a little boy got out. Alex walked around to the passenger side and opened the door. A woman got out and stood to kiss him on the lips. The kiss was of two people madly in love with each other. Her hair covered the side of her face, so I couldn't see her. Alex opened the back passenger door, and a little girl got out. As Alex bent down to pick the little girl up, the woman grabbed the little boy's hand, and they proceeded to walk in the direction of the restaurant. I finally saw her whole face as she looked left and right for traffic before crossing the street. It was Cynthia Black, aka Cynthia Pierson. He held his daughter and had his other hand around Cynthia's waist at this point.

I was stuck and shocked. I know my attorney said I don't have to get a divorce because I am technically not married, but I damn sure will be getting child support. I will most likely get about fifteen to twenty thousand a month. Also, I'll be keeping all the money in our banks that has my name on it. I've already moved everything to a personal account of mines. So, I hope this Bitch can take care of dinner tonight. He obviously doesn't know because he is smiling from ear to ear right now.

They walked into the restaurant, and I saw them be seated along with a few others. I couldn't see well, so I got out of the car and got closer. As I started to get closer and closer, I began to see the people at their table. It's his parents and her parents sitting with them. They were celebrating his mother's birthday, by the looks of it. Wow, so they are in on it too. That is when I just clicked and saw red. I had to say something.

The stride in my walk demanded everyone to move out of my way. When I approached the table, everyone looked at me, you can see all the color from their faces disappear, including Alex's. But the part that really sent me over the top was the smile on Cynthia's face that made her look like a damn Siamese cat. This Bitch!

"Zada? Umm, what are you doing here?" This muthafucka had some nerve. Right at that moment, the waitress came back to the table.

"Is everyone ready to order?"

"No, we are not. Please give us a moment."

"Yes, ma'am. Would you like a chair?"

"No, sweetheart, this won't take long at all." She turned and quickly walked away to give me my moment.

"What am I doing here? Well, let's see. I guess I was just driving through just to, I don't know, oh yeah, that's right! I wanted to see my husband, his first wife, his two kids and my lovely in-laws. But that's neither here nor there at this moment. I am here to let you know that you can have this life you so lovingly worked so hard at keeping a secret. I will be getting a divorce in Florida and would recommend that you do not step foot in my town, or I will have your ass arrested and thrown in jail for bigamy. So, stay your funky, corroded, one-minute sex having, ass backward, low life, stank breath, half-ass daddy, no-money-having-after-I-get-done-with-yo-ass, living off your wives, selfish son of a REAL Bitch, right here in UTAH where you belong! Just to let you know, you will be getting served with child support papers.

"That is all I needed to say. I hope you all have a great night. Enjoy your miscellaneous money while you can because I will be coming after you and your wife. You both will pay for my pain and suffering. So much for getting involved with a rich bitch. Oh, and by the way, your wife will be paying for this lavish dinner. Your account should be at around 0 right about now. Toodles!"

The looks on their faces were priceless. Alex was calling me as I walked away, but my ears can't hear bullshit no more. I felt good about what I just did. As I said what I said, Cynthia's smile wiped from her fucking face. Especially when I said I'll be going after both of them.

Chapter 36

ZANDRA ROZE ROYSS

You haven't heard from me in a while. I've been busy minding my own business. I have had a lot on my plate with the miscarriage and all. But we will talk about me later. So, well, well, well, I guess I have the greatest family in the world. Everyone is doing pretty good if you ask me. Let's start with my old-ass-trifling-abusive dad. He is somewhere out there in the world with my Uncle Zain, probably living it up with chicks and drinking himself into a coma. My mother is busy taking care of her precious fucking favorite son, Zandell. She is helping him consolidate his relationship with his newfound father. That bitch been lying all this time, and punk ass Zandell is ok with it. All of it. How in the fuck! But whatever, it's not my problem.

Zander Jr is living his best life after a crazy ass ex-girlfriend tried to take him out. She made his life miserable. I thought the shit was funny as hell. This negro thought that by being a damn ex-gigolo, he would be able to just walk right into marital bliss. Hahahaha, that fool was scared when that girl was fucking his shit up. His own girlfriend had to put their hands on her because my punk-ass brother wouldn't. Punk ass. Now he is getting married to Noel. Can you fucking believe it? Yes!!! She said yes to the fucking dress! Hahahahaha. Well, I guess my brother will have a lifetime bodyguard. Haahahaha. Dumb ass broad. Well, not all the way dumb because she's loaded with cash, and she is smart as hell. Ok, so I take back the dumb ass broad, but I will not take back the bodyguard. Hahahaha

Damn, this weed is hitting. I've been in the back of the house in my dad's corvette blazing up like a muthafucka all by myself. Now, this is the life. Plus, I am about to pop this Molly too! I'mma be higher than a bitch up in here.

Ok ok ok so let me get back to the greatest family in the world. So next on the family's list is my sister, Zada. She is about to start living the great life because she found her husband married with 2 kids. Hahaha!! She's not legally married to her idiot of a fake husband. She never liked his stupid ass, anyway, how could she. Alex is tall and handsome, don't get me wrong but he's boring as hell, he has no swag, and I am quite sure he can't fuck. I am sure. He looks like it.

Now Zada, she's very pretty and smart, she has everything a man wants. Plus, she's already rich! Anyone can see that she is a solid winner. Also, my beautiful sister got pregnant by one of the world's richest artists. Raphael Lovechild aka Ca$h! Fucking really!!! Keep up the great work sis! But I feel bad for her because I know this is not the life she wanted. But then again, I don't feel sorry for her because her ass shouldn't have married for the sake of what people thought was best for her. Oh well, you win some, you lose some.

Zaniyah, Zaniyah, Zaniyah. That girl right there, is a trip. She doesn't know that I have been to her dorm a few times and saw pictures of her and her friends out partying. I was being noisy and stumbled on some crazy pics. She is fucking girls and guys. Damn sis, what a way to live! I must give her her props because she is living that college life to the fullest. I am not hating on her because she has always been here for me, so I'll leave her alone, but she needs to be safe sleeping with everybody before her ass catch something she can't get rid of. Crazy ass girl.

Entering the left corner is Zandell!!! The crowd is going wild!!! Hahahahahhaa. Damn I'm funny. Talking to yourself is the best medicine. No one can argue or disagree with you. Anyhoo, so my brother Zandell is the golden child even when he beats people up and break their noses, he is the baby of all babies. He's athletically gifted and now we know why. He's a straight A student, he's handsome as all get out, and all the girls love him.

He's talks proper and doesn't curse unless he is upset or something, but other than that, he is a really sweet young man, and he doesn't bother nobody. I love him to death, but he hasn't been around lately because he has a new dad. He is happy and I don't blame him. I guess I am a little jealous in a way. Nahhhh I'm good all my myself.

Finally, it's yo girl, Zandra, baby!!! Hahaha I am here and in the flesh. I have meet me some new friends and I am living life better than anybody in the fam. I have found ways to not feel hurt, pain, or sorrow. I have gone through a true soul crushing experience and nobody seems to understand. I pretty much be at the house alone most of the time while Mom is out mending relationships; I guess she forgot about ours or that she even has a baby girl. I have been getting dropped off to school by her but that's it. I've hit a few parties here and there enjoying my free time. Mom hasn't been home much, so I have been chillin in dad's corvette riding around town. I am happy I know where he stashes his money in his office. I have to keep the gas tank good so I can do me.

I'm sorry that I don't have nothing going on with me right now. I am just talking and getting shit off my chest. I hang, grab what I need, get dad's money and go. That's it. I haven't been dealing with anybody. My Molly has been keeping me company. My mom said I need to see a shrink. Yeah right. I don't need one. I just want to be left alone. Alex calls to check up on me from time to time to see how I am feeling. My brother and Alex are still close, but Zandell has been busy getting to know his new family.

RING

"Yup."

"I'm at the gate."

"I'm on my way."

I drove my father's vette up to the front gate and hopped out to get my package.

"You got the money?"

"Here it is. Give me the package first."

"Look Lil girl, I call the shots. Give me my five hundred dollars, or I will drive the fuck off."

"Tough crowd, here." I gave him the money, he gave me my bag of pills and then left.

I got back in the corvette and drove to the back of the house again. I am going to take another

Molly and go to bed, I am tired.

My brother's wedding is in a week. I don't know why, but all my siblings are part of the wedding party. This is ridiculous. I don't want to be bothered, but I'll do it for his soft ass. Wearing flowers, bright colors and watching the smiles on everybody's faces because their lives are back in order? Yuck! Seriously? I have five more years to enjoy any piece of a real life. My freedom is still gone until I'm eighteen. I can't cut my brain off. I need to get to bed because school is tomorrow. It doesn't matter whether I go or not, no one cares about the loud and rude Zandra; the one who is always getting into trouble. It's funny that everyone feels that way because not one muthafucka sat down to ask me why. They just do what they can, to cover it up. They get me out of trouble with their money and then tell me what's best for me which is school and sports. Maaaan fuck school, fuck sports and fuck this family.

She parks the car and heads in the house. When she shuts the house back door and lock it, she feels a weird chill and it seems like she is being watched. She turned and looked out of the window, but no one was there. She ran upstairs and threw all her clothes off, popped a Molly and closed her eyes. She continued to think to herself as sleep started to take over her.

I hate my life. My daughter is dead, and I have nobody. I am alone and scared of this big world that everyone keeps hiding me from. I am scared, but I will never tell anyone that. If I would have had my daughter, I would've talked to her while she was in the womb, rubbed my belly, and told her how I'd make everything okay. I would have been the best mom, not like my mother or any of my sisters. They have ruined their kids' lives. I would have married Alex, and we would have raised our daughter the right way. Well, at least that's what I would have tried to do. I want to just scream; I want to get out of this skin, just run and never come back to this place.

The one person who I thought wouldn't desert me is my dad. Believe me, I am pissed at how he did my mom, but he always had my back. I looked up to him and how his presence filled a room. I secretly wanted to have my dad's power. But he left, and he hasn't called nor text me. He only reached out to Zada about the family business, and that was through a text. He's a coward. He just left. I could have gone with him. I feel like I want to just stop breathing. I don't want to live. I just feel……...so……… sad…….

Chapter 37

Zander Roze Royss Jr

I am getting married. I am the happiest man alive. I proposed in one of the most creative traditional ways. I invited the whole family along with her family to my house, and I popped the question and she said yes. I am not waiting long at all; Noel hired a wedding planner, and I am supposed to meet her today. She has some questions for me. I am not excited because I don't want to get involved in the planning, I just want to spend the money, and things just happen. However, she said the wedding planner insisted that she get my advice on some things because she wants this to be the perfect day for the both of us, not just Noel.

DING DONG

I hope this is quick because I have things that I have to do today.

I opened the door and stood like a statue; I couldn't move. Is this why the planner wanted to see me? Why the fuck is the world fucking with me?

"What the fuck are you doing here?

"It's nice to see you too." She bumped my shoulder as she brushed past me. Why fucking why!!!!!

"What the fuck are you doing here? I know damn well you knew you was talking to Zander Roze Royss Jr's future wife when you accepted this wedding planner gig. So why in the fuck did you except it, Pepper?" Yes, her fucking name is Pepper! She was the biggest hoe on campus. I took advantage and was in that ass every night.

"I am here to do a job; I am getting paid lovely. And I was not turning it down. If you don't tell, I won't tell. So just sit down, shut the fuck up and answer these got damn questions. Be happy that I requested to speak to you alone rather than in front of your wife." She said that with a disgusting look, but I saw the lust in her eyes!

"I'll be back." I stormed into the kitchen. I splashed water on my face and wondered why the hell am I tripping. I love the hell out of Noel. I suddenly looked down and saw my reasoning for being so damn jumpy; this chick can still make me rise. Shit, Shit, Shit. I relaxed and calmed my nerves. No fuck that. I don't want that bitch!

"Zander, are you coming any time in the near future?"

My penis finally went down. I knew it would because I have trained my body not to react to bitches. Right before I started to make my way back into the family room, I heard Noel.

"Hey Pepper, how is everything going? I left work early to be here. I wanted to help Zan with the questions you're going to ask him. You know how men are. You have to help them with these things. They don't really care about this stuff. Hahaha"

Oh, no problem, Noel, I am happy you are here."

Noel walked into the kitchen and smiled that smile that I fell in love with. "Hey, sexy." She put her juicy lips on mines and felt me up in the kitchen.

"Pepper, we are coming in a moment." Noel bellowed.

"Ok, no problem. Take your time." Pepper replied.

Noel started to unzip my paints and pull out my dick.

"Wooo babe, we have guest. Right now?"

"Yes, and right now, she can't see us."

She put her finger in my mouth to suck on, bent over with her ass in the air, and slid her lips over my dick with ease. Noel took my member in her hand and messaged my balls with the other. She knew exactly what to do to make me cum. She sucked me and was using her tongue on my head at the same time. I threw my head back because I was about to cum hard.

"Damn, this is what married life will be like?"

"I got you, baby."

She started sucking fast and harder like she was forcing the cum out of me.

"Zan, I want you to cum in my mouth."

"You do?"

"Yes, baby, I do."

I started to form that O with my mouth.

I tried to keep from getting loud.

"Fuck, here it cum, oh shit, shit," I whispered.

My wifey sucked every bit of my semen right down her throat. She sucked and licked me clean. I didn't have to dry off or nothing. My baby did that shit for me. Wow! My baby got skills. Thanks goodness!

She wiped her mouth, popped kiss me on the lips and gave me a succulent kiss on my neck that gave me chills. I am one happy man.

"Damn you taste good."

"Thank you." I sounded like a bitch. Oh well, I'll be a bitch for future wifey.

"Come on, babe, let's go and handle this situation with Pepper."

"Ok." I zipped up my pants and followed Noel like a puppy in heat. I didn't give a damn about Pepper no more.

The smile on Pepper's face said it all. She knew what happened, but I just kept my damn mouth shut and answered those damn questions.

After our meeting with Pepper, I tried to get me some ass, but Noel wasn't having it.

"Noel, go put on that red lace dress on that I like with no panties."

"No, remember? We are not having sex until our honeymoon night."

"Babe, come on. You just sucked my dick; you might as well go all the way."

"No, and I know who Pepper is."

I started choking off my own spit. Noel pat my back hard.

"What do you mean you know Pepper?"

"I know the whole story about you and Pepper. I didn't know she would be the one that the agency would send me, but she is very good at her job, and I wanted the best. I don't care about your history. But I am not a damn fool, so I made sure to be here."

"Who told you?"

"Ummmm, I have connections and don't worry about that. Anyways, no ass until the wedding night. Got it?"

"Got it. Can I kiss you?"

"Yes, you can."

I kissed the hell out of my future wife-to-be with her cum mouth and all. I don't give a fuck; it's mine.

Chapter 38

Zandell Roze Royss

What can I say? I have been living the life. School is about to be out, my brother is getting married next week, and I am his best man. I am happy for the guy. He deserves it. I am glad that he finally got it right. Noel is a cool chick, and she is smart too.

My dad and I have been kicking it hard, and he was invited to the wedding. I am happy because I can enjoy more time with him. We are trying to get to know each other on a personal level. It seems like my mom is trying to get cozy with him, and I don't know if I like that. I overheard Zada and Zaniyah talking one night while mom was washing up to go out. They were saying how she is moving on too fast, and sometimes when a woman has been with a man for a long time, they should take time with finding who they are first. A woman can take out her frustrations on a good man because she hasn't let the baggage go from the bad man she has had. I don't know that much about relationships, but from the looks of things, I agree with my sisters, and it seems to me that if the shoe fits, wear it. I just want my dad to myself. I just hope that she doesn't get in the way of things.

My dad is about to pick me up in a few, so I am trying to pick the right outfit to wear. I've been tripping with my haircuts and wardrobe. Creon has swag, and I am trying to mimic my dad, but his style is weird. I'll get it down soon.

RING

"Hey, Dad."

"I'm outside."

"Ok, I am on my way. I just have to say bye to someone."

"Ok, no problem.

"Hey Dad, will it just be us, my sister and brother, today?"

"Yes. Is everything ok?"

"Yes, I'll talk to you when I get in the car."

"Ok lil man."

"Cool."

I am so happy to be leaving this miserable place. Everyone around here has been depressed, stressed and doing their own thing. Since all the secrets are out, it's been really quiet. I am worried about one thing, though, Zandra. She has been in her room and hasn't been coming out or talking to anyone. She seems so depressed, and she won't talk to me. I have tried.

KNOCK KNOCK

"Zandra, can I come in, please?"

"Sure." I walked in and over to the bed. I sat on the edge beside her.

"Did you eat today?"

"At school."

"Are you ok? I'm worried about you."

"I'm good."

"Are you sure? I can ask Creon to let you tag alone if you want to get out of the house. Do you want to go with me? School is out. We can go shopping and spend his money. You know shopping always makes you feel better."

"No, that's ok, thank you, though." She leaned in and kissed my cheek. I smelled a little weed, but I know that she does that every now and then.

"Ok, if you say so. We are going to have fun. Creon is BBQing."

"No, you go ahead and enjoy your dad. I promise I'm good."

"I bet. Love you, sis." I kissed her forehead and got the heck out of that room. Mm, mm, mm, the depression in there is deep. I had to get out of there. I'll have to talk to my mom about this.

"What's up, Creon?"

"Hey, Zanny. What's good?"

"Everything."

We laughed and drove off. Creon started playing Ca$h song "Playboy" on his Bluetooth. I love leaving the mansion for some reason. I guess it's all the issues and having a family that wasn't free to speak their mind, makes me want to leave. Women scared, and men too weak to defend them. It was like an everlasting circle of fear. Just sad. Creon's family is cool and outspoken. They speak their minds, and he embraces it. I see what my mom saw in him. Oh yeah, that reminds me.

"Creon, can we talk about something that has been on my mind?"

"Sure, what's up?"

"My mom."

"What? Did something happen?"

"Woo Creon watch out for the curb!"

"My bad, is your mom, ok?"

"Yes, she is great. But this is why we need to talk. What is going on with you two?"

"Ok, um, well…."

"Creon just spit it out."

"Ok, your mother has always been the love of my life, and I would like to rekindle what we had. I couldn't have her at the time, and now, I want to see where it goes. Listen, son. I have always wanted to be a part of your life, so please do not think I am here because I only want to date your mom. That is not true.

I am solely here for you. However, your mother is a big part of that. But if you are not feeling it, please let me know. I want to know what you are thinking."

"Well, I don't mind that you are interested in my mom because she is a remarkable woman, and she will make someone very happy one day. But she is coming out of a troubling marriage, and she needs time to heal."

"Spoken like a true man, and yes, son, I promise that I am not rushing her at all. In fact, I told her I would wait for her. I asked her to be my friend because your mother told me the same thing you just said. Also, she said she wanted to wait until the divorce was final before dating. So, if I were you, I would be proud to have a mom like Ziola. She is thinking of you and all your brothers and sisters. She doesn't want to disappoint you guys any more than she already has. And me, I will do everything I can to not let you down. You just got into my life, and I don't want to jeopardize that in any way. Cool? Are you ok with your mom and I taking it slow by being friends for now?"

"Yeah, I'm fine with that. Can we also spend time without her as well? I am trying to get to know you, and when mom is around, you get the lovey-dovey eyes, and that irks me."

"Ok, deal. Thank you for understanding the care that I have for your mom. I will do nothing to hurt her. Promise."

"Cool. Because that was the next thing I was about to say. Don't hurt my mom."

"Ok. Haha, So I want to take us shopping for the wedding. Are you up for that?"

I nodded enthusiastically. "Definitely. I love to shop."

"Son let's have a father to son talk. I don't think you are but, if you are, its ok." Creon gave me a nervous look. I guess he is trying to figure out how to communicate with me. I am a straight shooter so it's easy. Just say it.

"Creon, I see that you are trying to figure me out with wanting to know about my personality, how I am as a person and other things. One thing that I am and from knowing you, I understand why, is that I am a straight shooter. Please just say what you have to say and if I am offended or not, I will let you know. Since you are my dad, I can trust that you wouldn't hurt me intentionally."

A smile of admiration spread across Creon's face.

"Son you are so smart. I absolutely love it. Ok, so with that being said, are you gay?"

I started choke coughing. No one has ever asked me that, but I guess it's fair. He doesn't know me, but what have I done for him to ask that. He started patting my back and had to pull over. He jumped out of the car and went to the back and got a Gatorade out of his cooler in the trunk.

"Are you ok son?"

I kept drinking until I caught my breath.

"Yeah, I'm good." He got back on the road.

"I tripped you up hard with that question, huh. Hahahahahaha." He damn sure did.

"Hahaha Ok, I am just saying if you were, I would love you regardless. That's all."

"Thanks, but no, I am straight."

"Ok, so do you have a girlfriend?"

"No, honestly, and I am not bragging or anything but, there are so many girls that like me, and it's to the point that I don't know if the feeling is genuine. Mom always says watch out for these girls because they are looking to get pregnant or just want to look good on a baller's arm. I told her I am only in high school, and it's not that serious, but mom don't care. She said these girls are starting out early with trying to trap you. I don't feel like dating right now for that reason."

"Your mother is right. I remember when I first went to the NBA. It was my first year in college, and when the NBA gave me an offer, your dad bounced. My name blew up. I was hot on the press. One night I walked into my hotel suite, and sure enough, a naked girl was laying in my bed. She looked every bit of seventeen. I was only 19 and man o man o man. I wanted the girl, but when I got on, my mother/your grandmother talked to me until I was blue in the face about girls like this. You can get charged for rape, statutory rape, get a girl pregnant etc.... So, I looked at the girl, thought about my mother's words, and decided that I loved my freedom and want to remain rich. So, your dad kicked her ass out naked and all. I didn't even let her put her clothes on. Hahahahaha. That was mean, but she was violating my privacy and to think she was trying to trap me? I just got in the pros. Give a brotha a chance to buy a house first."

My dad and I laughed and talked for hours. We went shopping in Tampa at the Greiner's Fine Men Clothing store. They knew Creon by name and treated him with the utmost respect. I know it's because he's a regular and he's rich. This is one of those high-end stores where Sr shopped. I never went shopping with Sr. He always bought my clothes and had them laid out on the bed for me or just had someone size me, get my suit tailored and delivered it to me. He never made time to be with me like this. Come to think of it, my dad and I never really spend father/son time together. I thought what we had was normal. He gave me money and bought me whatever I wanted. When he came to my games, I felt like that was the best thing popping.

Now I am experiencing what a father/son relationship is all about. As the man in the store started to size me, Creon explained to me all about the special things a man should know about a suit. Something as simple as not sagging, of course, but button the shirt to the top, unfasten the buttons on your jacket when you sit, the shoulders of my suit should hug my shoulders, and never wear a sports watch when you are wearing your suit. Creon was talking to me like we have been father and son since I have been born. I kind of cried inside because I probably would have felt better being me if I knew he was my dad from the jump. I feel like I missed out.

When the man was done sizing me, I guess my emotions got the best of me. I left abruptly, went into the nearest bathroom and locked the door. Creon came after me.

"Zandell, what's up. Are you ok?"

"I need a minute." I couldn't let him see me like this. Oh man, I am acting like a bitch.

"Zandell, let me in, please. We need to talk; I want to make sure you are ok."

I wiped my tears and slowly opened the door. He locked the door back and walked me over to the couch.

"Zandy, talk to me... tell me what's up. Have you been crying?"

"No," My sniffle confirmed the lie.

"Ok, you have, and it's ok, but I need to know why. Tell dad what's up."

I told him everything. All my feelings, how I feel like I missed out on a great dad and a great relationship. Even all the way up to my attitude, it might have been different if he was in my life.

"I should have known about you. I just feel like I've missed out, that's all. I should have known about everything you are teaching me today."

"Ok, I feel you, son. And since I have heard everything that is on your mind, now let me tell you how I feel about that. I'm about to drop some stuff on you, so keep up." Both of us smiled. "Instead of thinking that you've missed out on something, think about what you have gained. You didn't have me, and that's not cool, but what if you did? You talked about your attitude, well that attitude that you have, you got that from me. My attitude was bad back in the day. When I knew I was rich and could get away with anything, my attitude became nasty, and I had no regard for peoples' feelings. Even today, I have people who hate my guts even though I have apologized, and I have changed. I can't believe I'm about to say this, but Sr was what was best for you at the time because he was mild-tempered, so we all thought, but you get my drift. He gave you a different view of how to deal with people and life. Remember the story you told me about when you got into that fight at school, and they tried to kick you out?"

"Yes, I remember."

"See? That was the manly way to handle that situation. Now, I would have handled it manly, but I would have had a different approach. However, coming into my life now, after I have grown, and matured allows me to be the best for you. So never look at this as a bad thing. Look at the good in it. Plus, you are about to be sixteen in a week. You are so young; we have time now and forever. Just imagine if you were twenty-six in the pros and here, I come talking about, "Oh that's my boy," you would look at me like I am crazy. Always remember, and hopefully, this will help you feel better. I have always been there. You have felt me be there too, you just didn't know it. And I promise if I had seen you about to fall at any time, I would have been right there to catch you. Do you understand where I am coming from?"

"I do. And I understand, thanks, Creon. I needed to hear that; I feel better now."

"Good. So, let's get you done and out of here so we can get something to eat. I love you, son. You don't have to say it back. I just wanted you to know that."

"It's all good. I love you too." He put me in a choke hold, and we played for a minute, then walked out of the bathroom to wrap up the fitting. I have to ask him later what he meant about me feeling him even when he is not around. I have been feeling like someone has been watching me. It's weird that he said that. Hmmm, I'll ask about that later.

THE FAMILY CHAPTER

Chapter 39

ZANDER ROZE ROYSS JR'S WEDDING

The Roze Royss Family has a beautiful day ahead as today was the day for Noel's and Zander Jr's wedding. The Backyard décor was radiant in its soft pink, lavender, and white colors with a sprinkle of silver. There were a hundred and fifty guests invited to the wedding. The chairs had pink, lavender and white coverings with lace silver ribbons tied to the back. There were roses spread about, with doves in white cages ready to be released after they were announced, husband and wife. The flowers were pink, lavender, and silver which was lined up on the left and right side of the isle for the bride. The walkway for the bride was decorated the same colors of her wedding, from the house all the way to the reverend. Food was laid out on the buffet tables for everyone. The appetizers were a roulade of chicken breast with fruit salad, French beans, scallions and orange salad. The salads on the side were garden salad with any dressing of their choosing. Entrees consisted of a seafood spread with snow crabs, shrimp, scallions wrapped in bacon. The entrees on the side for those who don't eat seafood, was baked chicken, string beans, white rice and mac and cheese. The spread was amazing. This is what they wanted, and everything was perfect. The wedding was taking place in an hour. Everyone was talking and smiling, looking for the event ahead. All the Roze Royss family was there, including Creon, Beverly, the triplets, all of Sr's family, Ziola's family, friends and enemies. However, Sr and Zain were not present.

Zandell Roze Royss

Today is here, and it's my birthday. I'm sixteen, and my brother is getting married. It is a great day, but Sr is not here. Who could blame him? He's been gone for months now. It's like he doesn't exist. I'm glad it's not one of my sisters getting married because my mother would be walking them down the aisle all by herself. It's a shame that he's such a coward that he can't face his family. I'm glad Zada got the family business on lock because the business would have folded if we solely depended on my dad. At least he taught one of us something. I need to check on Zandra to see if she's almost ready.

Knock Knock

"Come in." My sister was in high spirits today, and I am so happy because I was worried. I guess weed does help in some ways. She has been on it every day.

"Hey sis, dang, you smell good. What are you wearing?"

"Dolce Gabbana Light Blue and thanks."

"So, just like we discussed."

"I know I know, no weed today. I wouldn't dare. Today is a beautiful day for love and people making their wishes come true."

"I'm happy to see that you're in good spirits. You had me worried there for a minute."

"No worries, Bro. Everything will be great from here on out. Promise."

She has done a 360. This is crazy but I'll take it.

"Ok, so hurry up and get downstairs."

I kissed my sister on the forehead and left to get in place. It's now 30 minutes to starting time. I want to be prepared because I'm going to a party after this.

Alexis is the flower girl, Zandra, Zaniyah, and Zada are bridesmaids. Noel's sister is her maid of honor. She's pretty too. We are not related, so I can get with that. She's eighteen, though. But who cares? I don't. She's been giving me the eye all day. I am Jr's best man and looking fresh to death.

Zada Roze Royss

Well, Raphael is coming to the wedding. I want the world to know who I am with. I'm single and ready to move on officially. It's weird to say this, but I've never been married. That is too funny. I guess things happen for a reason. I'm showing now, five months, and this is the first time I'm enjoying being pregnant. Once Alex found out I was having a girl, he started to treat me differently, but not Raphael. He is so attentive and caring. We just found out yesterday that we are having a boy. He is so elated. I am too.

"Hey, beautiful." Omg!!! I love this giddy feeling I get when he comes around.

"You came!"

"Of course. Anything for you." I started to hear whispers from people saying that it's Ca$h.

"So, I guess everyone's having something to say about us. They are whispering."

"So. Are you nervous?"

"Just a little. Everyone has always seen me with Alex."

"Ok, so maybe this will calm you a little." He put his hand on the back of my head to bring me to his lips, and he kissed me like I have never been kissed before. When his soft lips danced with mine, I forgot about the world.

"Look, mommy their kissing. I didn't know you kiss with your tongue. You and daddy don't do that."

Raphael and I started giggling at the little boy, who was the son of my mother's friend. When I looked at her, she winked at me. I was on cloud nine. I can't wait until this wedding is over. I am going to tear him up. Twenty minutes until the wedding.

Zaniyah

Look at my Freaky ass sister tonguing down a celebrity at her own brother's wedding in front of everybody with her nasty ass. I hate her! I'm so jealous! Hahahaha, you go sis. She deserves it. I'm so happy that Alex's ass ain't coming back with his little dick self. I would never say a word, and I would take it to my grave. I remember when I would spend the night with my sister in my early college days, and I would hear them. I'd sneak out of the guest bedroom, crack their door just a little bit and watch them fuck. Oh man it was fun. I think Alex saw me watching one time because he was lame as hell any other time but that one time he performed like a champ. My sister was on top doing her thing, he had his hands on her thighs, not doing shit, but he saw me, so he put his hands on her ass, started pumping up in her and going crazy. She looked happy because she told him to fuck her harder. He flipped her on her back and put her in the buck and fucked the shit out of my sister.

Omg!!! Did I just get excited about my sister fucking? I need sex bad. This is ridiculous. I can't have sex for a while because I contracted chlamydia and had to take doxycycline twice a day for fourteen days. I found out that my so-called boyfriend and Keisha have been having threesomes with other people and the muthafuckas brought me back an STD. My discharge went from clear to fucking green. Maaaaaan, I fucked them two up. They had to call the police at my dorm. I've decided on who I am going to deal with going forward. I'm sticking with my men. I need to stop kidding myself. I love to get dicked down. Especially watching my sister tongue down her boyfriend and me daydreaming about her screwing her so called ex-husband. This is stupid. But chlamydia told me to sit my ass down and that's what I'm doing.

I'm getting in position to walk down this damn aisle, and as soon as I'm done, I'm going to take off this gown that I am wearing, tie up my pretty afro, then get in a nice warm bubble bath, put on some Ms. Jonez Jody Macc, rub on my clit soft and slow while using my other hand's finger to insert her in my va jay jay as far as she will go. Then masturbate as many times as I can. FUUUUUUCK!! This wedding needs to hurry the fuck up!!!

Zander Jr

I'm nervous as shit standing out here in this hot ass suit. My palms are sweating, and my best man be looking sharper than me because his collar is dry.

"Ok, Jr, you are tripping. Relax, dry off your forehead, man. Dang, she is the woman of your dreams, right?"

I nodded. "Yes, she is. I'm just nervous as shit."

"Shhhhh the reverend is right there."

"I don't give a shit about the reverend, I'm the one getting married. Damn, why am I so nervous." My brother passed me his handkerchief.

"Here take this and wipe off your face. I promise when you see her, you will relax."

"Damn, when did you get so smart?"

"Watching all of yawl, plus, I'm only imaging how I would feel if I was your shoes."

"Ok whatever. Just be careful. I saw Noel's sister looking at you. Stay away from her. She loves athletes. Hahahaha."

"Really cute."

"Zandell, is that dad and Uncle Zain?"

"Wow, it sure is."

My brother and I walked away from the Rev after my father and Uncle found their seats up front.

We hugged dad and dapped Uncle Zain.

"Dad, I'm glad you could make it. The wedding is running a little late as expected, but did you want to walk mom down the aisle?"

"Sure! I didn't know if you'd want that."

"Of course, I can put all that to the side. She is in the foyer. Hurry because we are about to start."

"Ok, thanks, son." He jetted off to make it. The music was getting queued to start.

Ziola Roze Royss

I saw Zander Sr running up the runway. My heart skipped a beat because of the love I thought I still had for him. He looked refreshed and as handsome as ever. But everything fled back to me, and I remembered everything. Fuck Sr.

"Hello, Ziola."

"Hi, Sr. I thought you were in Canada. Yes, I know every move you make, I have my ways. We are still married but not for long."

"Ziola, I'm only here for our son. He asked me to walk with you. I am not here to hurt you. I promise I'll leave right after the ceremony."

The music started to play, and I knew this walk would be over in a second. He's just walking me to my seat. I stuck out my elbow for him to grab, he was finally able to breathe, and we walked with grace down the aisle. As we got to my seat and Zander Sr was about to sit me, I heard a piercing scream from the house. It sounded like Zaniyah. After the scream, I heard Oh My God repeatedly. I kicked off my heels and started running towards the scream. The family started running behind me to see what the fuck was going on. I hopped up two stairs at a time with everyone on my heels. The screams were coming from Zandra's room. I bust the door open, and what I Saw......... Left......... Me......... Speechless...

Chapter 40

ZANDRA ROZE ROYSS

Now I lay me down to sleep, I pray the lord my soul to keep, if I shall die before I wake, I pray the lord my soul to take.

As I lay in my sister's arm, she tries to shake me awake. She screams Oh My God. But it's too late. I told my brother something today. Peoples' dreams will come true, and my 50 Mollies did exactly that for me.

White puss with bubbly foam started rolling out of the side of my mouth. Zaniyah freaked out, so she quickly wiped it off to do mouth to mouth. Wow, she really loves me. I saw a glimpse of Zada crying and calling the police while Noel stood and stared at me like bitch, how dare you do this shit on my wedding day, your brother's birthday, you selfish ass spoiled little brat. I wish I would have known that they loved me so much because maybe I would have changed my mind. Maybe I would have talked to someone or screamed at someone for not seeing the pain that I was going through.

Zaniyah

"What the fuck! Zandra!" I looked at the remaining pills lying on the bed. "What the fuck did you take??? Zada!!!!!!! HELP!!!!"

Zada

Zada walked in my room toward the yelling. "Why the hell are you yelling? What the fuck!" I looked stunned at first because I couldn't believe my eyes. Pills all over the bed, Zaniyah was yelling and trying to perform CPR.

"She took Mollies, and I don't know how many! Call 911!!!" Zaniyah saw Zandra fade out, so she started shaking her. She rolled her on her side and wiped the inside of her mouth.

"Zandra, how could you!!!! What the fuck!!!! She's fucking foaming out the mouth!!! Tell them to hurry!!! Zada don't just stand there. Call 911!!!!"

Zada

"My sister just took a bunch of pills. My address is 36455 Bayshore Blvd Tampa!! Yes, that's the address!!! Hurry, she is foaming, out of the mouth!!!!"

Zaniyah

Zandra's body started to convulse, and I felt my entire body stiffen.

"Oh shit, I'm losing her!!! Zandra!! Zandra!!!"

"OH MY GOD!!!!! OH MY GOD!!!!! NOOOO NOOOO NOOOO!!! Zandra!!!! NOOOOO!"

Zada

I dropped the phone, ran to Zandra, and started CPR with Zaniyah.

"NOOOOOO, WHY DID YOU DO THIS!!!!"

Noel bust in the room and couldn't move. She heard muffles from the floor and saw the phone.

"Ma'am, are you there? Ma'am!"

Noel jumped out of her daze and picked up the phone.

"Um, hello." She was in shock. Things were moving so fast. Next thing you know, Ziola runs in the room.

"Operator, I think she's gone. Do you have the address?"

"Yes, Ma'am, the ambulance is on the way. Just say with me."

Noel couldn't. She just put the phone down. Everyone ran to the bed, but Noel couldn't move. She was still in shock. Everyone was crying and yelling. The sirens were close; she could hear them. Holy fucking shit. This girl did not kill herself. Why didn't she come to any of us? This family. This poor fucking family. They can't catch a break.

The EMT finally got there and tried to revive her, but she was gone. Ziola fell to the floor and cried like she had never cried before. She didn't see it. She was so worried about her own fucking life; she didn't realize that her daughter's life was draining from her. Noel saw paper on the side of the bed during the commotion, a letter to the family by Zandra. She folded it and put it in her bra. After everyone is settled and calm, she'll read it. She knows that no one else will have enough strength to do it.

The Roze Royss Family went to the hospital only to get it confirmed that Zandra Roze Royss completed her mission in suicide at the age of thirteen. The family couldn't do anything else but go home. The house was very quiet, everyone sat in the family room speechless on what just happened.

Zaniyah

I sat in the chair, looking into space as tears softly slid down my face. I still had leftover white hardened puss on my cheek from trying to revive my baby sister. Why would she do this? I failed her.

Zada

I held onto Zaniyah as I looked into space and let my thoughts overtake me. I'm the big sister, and I know I had my own mess going on, but I wasn't paying attention. She wanted to watch Alexis for me so many times to probably have the love of a baby around because she lost hers and I was too busy running around tending to my own fucked up business to notice her pain. My shit could have waited until she was straight, at least. I failed her.

Zander Jr

On my wedding day, Zandra! Really! I will never forget this! Why would you do this to everyone? You could have come to anyone of us at any time. Anytime! I can't take this. I am having a family meeting and asking everyone that's here, if there is a fucking issue, please speak your got damn mind. My sister felt like she had no one to turn to with all of these people in this room who loves her unconditionally. That means we just fucking ignored her altogether. Fixing our own shit and not helping the young minds who don't know what to do about handling stress. We are fucking grown; we can handle it or find a way because we have experience, or we have grown tough enough skin over time to be strong enough for these things. We can't expect a child to overcome something like this without guidance.

Zandell

I knew it, and I saw her falling, and I wasn't there to pick her up. I saw the desperation on her face. I saw it, I fucking saw it. I need to relax before I blow. She was my best friend. Why didn't she come to me? Why? I'm fucking pissed at Zandra because she knew that I would have been there for her. Fuck! Relax relax relax relax.

Zander Sr

Well, if anyone has a finger pointed at them, it's me. I was a coward to leave my family behind to let them deal with what I did all on their own. I am so stupid, and I can't even say anything because I should have been here to help mend the pieces. I left the burden on their mother to handle the household and my shit. I have no words to say to justify anything. I am just speechless. This is a loss that will leave a hurt on everyone forever. I feel like I am dying inside. I love you, Zandra, and if you can hear me, Daddy is so so sorry.

Ziola

How could I not see it or felt this was going to happen? It's obvious when these things happen that a person should get help. She was thirteen screaming for attention. Pregnancy, bad grades, fighting, leaving the house at night and so on and so on. I knew she was getting out, but she didn't go far. This family don't know but I had hired a private detective for the family. My family feel like their being watched and I laugh because they are.

This is how I know what they are always up to. I found a detective to watch over them due to our family's status. I needed to make sure that my babies were all right. I hired my PI years ago, but recently, I decided to stop the services. My family was safe from what I can see, and I felt a PI was no longer needed. However, little did I know, my problems were far worse now verses back then. This is a mess; my PI would have seen this coming. My soul is crying, it's broken, and I have no strength to fix it; nor, do I want to.

But now we are here, and she is gone. I am the worst mother ever. How can I move on from this?

This family is torn because of me not standing on my own two feet and having a fucking backbone. Not standing up to people and speaking my mind. Not protecting my children. OMG!! Zandell. This is going to destroy him. They were best friends. I am glad that Creon is here. He is sitting with Zandell because he knows his son is like him, and anything can pop off. I single-handedly destroyed my family. I feel dead inside.

Noel stood up to make an announcement.

"Um everyone, I know that this is a very bad time, but while everything that was going on, I found a note from Zandra addressed to the family. I wanted to wait until we were all here to read it. I haven't read it; this will be my first time. I would like to read it for you. However, if anyone wants to do it instead, just say the word."

Noel waited a moment, and just as she expected, nobody moved. She nodded her head and took a deep breath because this was hard for her too.

Chapter 41

THE LETTER

To My Beautiful Roze Royss Family,

I know you all are upset with my choice to call it quits and leave this beautiful earth. I am so sorry that I had to hurt you all, but I just could not take it anymore. I was mad with all of you, but I am not anymore. If you are reading this letter, that means I have moved on to a better place. I am with the angels now. I know how I went out wasn't the coolest, but I am a child. That should count for something. Right? I guess I'll find out. My cries for help went unanswered, and I am sorry, but I had to do what I felt was best for me. You may not agree, but I had to do what my heart called me to do. You will think what I did was selfish, but everyone had their own lives. I just felt like I was a burden, and I am sorry that you may feel different. I know I am gone physically, but I will always be in your hearts. Don't be mad at me, please. I know I am young, but I had a lot on my soul to where I would have had to do a lot of work to heal. I was ready to go, and I am ok with that. Again, you may not agree but now you all can get your lives together. Promise me you will, I am now out of the way. Literally. Hahaha. I know you don't find that funny so let me get back to being serious. Sorry for the bad joke.

Hey Jr, I know you are beating yourself up about all of this, how you missed it and so on, but you didn't miss anything. You were focusing on your soon-to-be lovely wife. I believe she is going to make you so happy. Make sure to name your daughter after me because I will not be there, and you will need something to remember me by. How will you forget me, though! Hahahahaha. I want you to know that you are a great big brother, you handled your business, and you couldn't have known that I was hurting. You were hurting too with your anxiety and all. I hope you continue to keep that under control because that is a killer.

But I wish you all the happiness in the world and a sound of advice, if you stop cheating on these girls, you will have a more happier path. So don't mess around on Noel. I really like her, and she can fight. I heard what she did at your house to Lavender. You have a hood chick! Great pickings, Bro! Keep making her happy and tell her to not hurt you either. Since I am not there anymore, believe me, I will haunt her but, first I have to find out how to do that, but it won't take me long. Hahahahaha. Noel I love my brother. Sorry for the jokes. Come on, yawl know I am a jokester. Ok, I am using my serious face now before Jr is getting mad. I love you so much Jr, never forget that. Kisses to you.

My Zada. Ohhhhhh girl, not really married to the scumbag huh!! Good for you. I don't have a lot of experience, but I am smart. Plus, I am an honor roll student, so believe me when I say that I understand what I hear. So good for you, Sis. You didn't need him. You are a smart woman who Dad left his business to. If you couldn't handle that business, Dad would not have let you be within 50 feet of it. I hope I said that right. Hahahahaha. What I want to say to you is that you have always been there for me. I asked to watched Alexis a lot because I just wanted to spend time with you two before this moment came. However, I loved our time that we had already. I remember all the life lessons you taught me. About boys, school and how to never let a man control you or your dreams. It sounds like you were talking about yourself, but to me, and I was fine with that. I want you to have fun and enjoy your life however you feel fit. You are dating Raphael, aka Ca$h. I am so happy about that. You have someone that can tear Alex butt up. Hahahahaha. I'll haunt Alex too if he tries anything, so send up a prayer if he messes with you. Sorry for the bad joke. Um, so back to your new love. Have fun. You're so uptight. Loosen up a bit, curse sometimes. I am quite sure Raphael got you thuggin it out a little bit. Or he may just like the good girl in you. Yuck! I don't even what to think about it. But anyhoo, I love you Sis and don't be mad. I am happy where I am, I promise. Kisses to you. Kiss Alexis for me and tell her that her Aunty is sorry but in a better place.

Zaniyah, there is so much to say, but I'll keep it short. I knew outside of Zandell, you would be the first to enter my room. If I am wrong, then I apologize, but I know you are always coming to get me when Zandell is not yelling at me to hurry up. You have done everything you were supposed to. You never failed at being the one person I can talk to, and I did not tell you what was going on because you would have tried everything to stop me. I did not want that. I just want you to remember all our good times together. I remember when you use to sneak and give me a shot of your Alize' and when you would buy me clothes that you know would piss mom off. Mom don't be mad; she was just doing what sisters do. Hahahahaha but I *did like the Alize' though. Hahahahaha. But Sis, you are the funniest sister in the world. Don't beat yourself down because you or no one could have stopped this. I had more than enough time on my hands, and it would have been done regardless. Just remember the good times, Sis. I love you so much, and please settle down and meet a nice guy. You deserve it. I hope you are handling that Chlamydia situation. Oops, my bad, yawl didn't know. Sorry Sis I had to jab you one last time. Hahahahaha Mom calm down and don't look at her like that. She has medicine for it. I bet Zaniyah is pissed right now. Sorry Sis, mom needs to know so you two can talk and maybe she can help you do better with being safe. I don't want you to catch something that you can't get rid of. Mom, she needs birth control because, she does not need a baby before her time. Learn from me big sis. Losing a baby is not fun nor is it forgettable, so please, Zaniyah do right and stay safe. Again, I love you Sis and keep your head up. Look at me being all mature and stuff. Hahahahaha. Rough crowd, rough crowd.*

Zandell, I love you so much, and you are my very best friend. I know you are wondering why I didn't come to you. Well, when I looked at your face over and over, I saw the joy Creon brought out in you when I saw that you were now learning where you came from and who you really are. I was so excited for you, and I didn't want to darken your light. I wanted you to continue to shine. Now you have a little sister and brother, and I want you to watch over them just like you did me. I'll always remember the parties' mom made you take me to. If you knew what I did at those parties when you weren't looking, you and Mom would have killed me first. Sorry, another bad joke. But you get my drift. Anyhoo, happy birthday and

I am sorry it was on your day, but our big head brother decided to get married on the same day. Everyone was going to be at the house, so I chose today, and I am so sorry for that. But you did nothing wrong, and there was nothing you could have done. You did it all already, which was to be the best brother a sister could have. I love you bro and stop dressing up for your dad. He will love you with whatever you wear. You be looking like a square. Hahahahaha. Sorry, I know you're not in a laughing mood. I love you forever, bro.

Finally, Mom and Dad. First, I want to say that you were the best parents that you could be. Yes, there were mistakes made, people were hurt, and things could have been different, but you two really did what you thought was best. Everyone makes mistakes, and even though there are parenting books for you to read, I am quite sure the experience is totally different; and not as easy as it seems. And to let you know, coming from me, Zandra Roze Royss, the books got nothing on your parenting skills. I was a spoiled pain in the butt. You still took care of me and disciplined me. You never gave up on me, so please do not beat yourselves down about me leaving. It's just that I was tired. I am an overly smart girl who was about to have a baby and was given the best advice from my family and friends. I have lived long enough, it just got too much, and I really felt alone. In my mind, I had to remove myself, and I did. I am so sorry I hurt you. Over time it will get better, at least that's what I think. I really made you guys work hard, and I didn't mean to, I just wanted all the attention, and I didn't think about anyone else. That wasn't fair. So, I am sorry to all my siblings. Period. Dad, find solace in Beverly. It seems that you really care for her. Mom, allow Mr. Creon to sweep you off your feet again. Don't get mad with Zandell, but he told me that Creon is crushing on you. I think you should go for it, Mom. Please do whatever makes you happy because you will need someone to be there for you during this trying time. I sure don't want you and Dad to console each other. That would be a catastrophe. Hahahahaha. Sorry, too soon? Probably. Ok, back to my serious face. You may not believe that you were there for me because of what I did, but you where there when I needed you. I love you, Mom, and I love you too, Dad. Thank you both for believing in me. I hope you find happiness because I sure have. Again, I love you both. Oh yes, and by the way. I have six copies of this letter in my top vanity draw. So, Mom, you can give everyone their own copy.

Ok, fam, that's my time. Literally. Hahahahaha. Again, too soon? Yup! Again, my apologies. I love all of you so much, and I know you are hurting, but it will be ok. Everyone make love tonight! On me! Nope. That came out wrong. Scratch that! Hahahahaha. Everyone just love each other and be there for each other. Watch and see who may need you and be there for them.

Continue Sunday dinners but this time, be genuine and really have fun, talk at the table, sing at the table, wear shorts, sundresses, shades, occasionally burp. Nope, don't do that. But you get my drift. Just be yourselves and be free. Big kisses to all of you. Go shopping with the life insurance money, on me. Now that was a good one. Love you!!! Kiss Kiss Kiss

From Your Loving Daughter, Sister and Friend

Everyone in the room was quiet, and Noel walked up to Ziola and gave her the letter. There were moments when everyone giggled and laughed a little, but there was not a dry tear in the house in the end. Whether someone boo hoo cried, or just tears fell in silence, everyone was emotional.

Chapter 42

ZANDER ROZE ROSS JR

One year later.

"Hey babe, come on down! The family is here."

I watched my beautiful pregnant wife of twins' wobble down the stairs. We were having her gender reveal party. Our marriage was going well, and all was good, just like Zandra wanted.

"Ok, I am here. Those stairs are something else."

"Don't worry. I have the guest room ready for you in your last months. We got this. Come on, give me your arm."

I walked Noel out back, where all the tables were lined up. Tables and streamers, with food were all set up for the reveal. I was happy where everyone was in their lives. I had thought with losing Zandra, everyone was going to break, but it brought the family closer than ever. Mom is happy with her husband, Creon. She looks happy too. I have never seen her this radiant with my father. The same with my dad. Everyone took Zandra's advice. He got married to Beverly. She finally had her babes. Yes, she had twin boys. My dad has a lot of parenting to do. Good thing he's finally retired. He will need time off.

My sister Zaniyah and Zada have taken over the real estate business. Zaniyah has become the South's top real estate agent. She brought a new and exciting flavor to the company, and business is booming. They are doing better than my dad. Hahahahaha. She also opened her own dancing studio for girls ages six to twelve. She is busy, and she is on birth control. Hahahahaha She is talking to a guy but hasn't brought him around yet. She's waiting until the time is right.

Now, Zada is doing great. She's not married to Raphael yet, but I see it coming. Really soon. As far as Alex, at the moment, she is getting 30k a month for child support. But believe me, my sister didn't need the money. She moved off the estate and moved in with Raphael. It's best, the memories in that house weren't good for her. Alexis is coming around to liking Raphael, and little Raphael Jr is lucky to have these two as his parents. She looks happy these days, just like mom. It's funny. They were going through it with their husbands together, they are relieved and happy together. It's crazy how life works. Alex isn't coming back because he will get arrested on the spot, he FaceTime his daughter frequently. My sister still wants his daughter in his life.

Now, as far as Zandell, he started to mess up. He gave up on ball and dabbled a little with some drugs. He took Zandra's death the hardest, but we got him some help because we started seeing the signs early, now he is back on the team with a clear head and doing better than he did before. He will go to the NBA for sure. We are proud of him.

My parents opened a foundation in my sister's name to help troubled teens who have nowhere to go and no one to talk to. It's called, "Zandra Roze Royss Foundation." I am running the foundation for them, and I am loving it. Noel is doing it with me, too, and we are closer than ever. She has been my rock through it all.

My Uncle Zain married that model he claimed was just a booty call. Hahahahaha. She is young, but she doesn't want any kids right now, so they are always traveling and doing things until the day comes, and he is here today to witness the genders.

"Everyone grab your streamers!"

"Ten, nine, eight, seven, six, five, four, three, two, one!!!!!!!"

BOOM!!!!!!!

Pink and Blue confetti burst out of the streamers.

"A boy and a girl. My son will be Zander the III, and my daughter will be named after her Aunt Zandra."

Everyone jumped for joy. There were some tears of sadness as well, some didn't agree. One being Zandell, who said let it go, but I am honoring my sister's wishes. I think Zandell is not out of the dark yet. But this family will not lose him like we did Zandra. Everybody stays up in his ass. Including his dad.

"Zandell, are you good? I know you didn't agree with the name Zandra. But I had to grant our sister's wishes."

"You know, I thought about it, and I think it's a great idea."

"Really?"

"Yeah, I do. Don't worry about me. I see that look in your eyes, and I promise you that I am good man. Hahaha"

"Ok, I just want you to know that I love you, and I am always here for you. Do you hear me?"

"I hear you."

"Ok, let's go get some cake Knucklehead." I grabbed him in a chokehold. Well, I guess I stand corrected. My brother is coming around. Slowly. Slow progress is better than none. I love my crazy ass, silly ass, sad-ass, happy ass Roze Royss Family. Hahahahahahaha. I love you, Sis. We finally did it and pulled together like a family, just like you asked. Kisses to you.

Zander Jr and Zandell walked off to enjoy the family and embrace the excitement of the twins. The family has finally created a bound that no one can touch nor tear down.

If you are in a crisis, please call the National Suicide Prevention lifeline.

American Foundation for Suicide Prevention

www.Afsp.org
1-800-273-(talk) 8255

Made in the USA
Columbia, SC
22 December 2022